The Royal Mess

The Royal Mess

MaryJanice Davidson

KENSINGTON PUBLISHING CORP.
http://www.kensingtonbooks.com

BRAVA BOOKS are published by

Kensington Publishing Corp.
850 Third Avenue
New York, NY 10022

All Kensington titles, imprints and distributed lines are available at special quantity discounts for bulk purchases for sales promotion, premiums, fund-raising, educational or institutional use.

Special book excerpts or customized printings can also be created to fit specific needs. For details, write or phone the office of the Kensington Special Sales Manager: Kensington Publishing Corp., 850 Third Avenue, New York, NY 10022. Attn. Special Sales Department. Phone: 1-800-221-2647.

ISBN-13: 978-0-7582-1208-5
ISBN-10: 0-7582-1208-9

First Kensington Trade Paperback Printing: September 2007
10 9 8 7 6 5 4 3 2 1

Printed in the United States of America

Author's Note

As with *The Royal Treatment* and *The Royal Pain*, I've taken liberties, and as of this writing, Alaska still is not a country. However, it is possible to spend a wild night with a charming lady and, occasionally, bastard princesses do result.

The events of this book take place two years after the wedding of HRH Prince Sheldon, American citizen, to HRH Princess Alexandria, House of Baranov.

This book is for my father, Alexander Davidson III. He is not the inspiration for King Alexander II; he is King Alexander II. I have received praise I do not deserve for making up such a colorful monarch. The truth is, all I did was observe my father for three decades and write down what I remembered.

Acknowledgments

Thanks as always to Kate Duffy, supreme-o editor of the multiverse. She is unfailingly patient, never runs out of clever ideas, and best of all, thinks I'm great.

And to Ethan Ellenberg, my agent, for setting up the deal and generally keeping me out of trouble as I juggle various obligations.

Also thanks to the wonderful flap copy writers and cover designers at Brava. I can't write decent flap copy (the blurb on the back of the book) with a gun in my ear, and I've noticed that without a nice cover and intriguing flap copy, you could write the next *War and Peace* and it'll just sit on the shelves. Not that this is the next *War and Peace*. Or even the next *Gone with the Wind*. But still. You see what I mean.

My name's on the front, so if you like this book, I'll get the credit. But all I did was cough up a manuscript; the finished product was a group effort.

Basically, this book is for the unsung heroes of publishing—the ones who worked just as hard as I did, but whose names aren't on the cover.

"Bastard, adjective: Born to parents who are not married to each other: baseborn, illegitimate, misbegotten, spurious, unlawful."

—*Roget's II: The New Thesaurus, Third Edition. 1995*

"You are a pest, by the very nature of that camera in your hand."

—Princess Anne, to a photographer, quoted by John Pearson, in *The Selling of the Royal Family*

"If God made me a princess, why didn't he take a little more time and make my hair so it wouldn't snarl?"

—Robert N. Lee, Rowland V. Lee, Princess, Tower of London, while the Princess's mother is combing her hair, 1939

"Your life doesn't run you. You run your life."

—Alexander Davidson II

"What?"

—MaryJanice Davidson

Prologue

April 26, 2007

Dear King Alexander,

My name is Nicole Krenski, and I am your illegitimate daughter. My mother was Tanya Krenski; she was formerly a bartender at the Suds Bucket, which is where you met. You saw her socially for about three weeks before you married Queen Dara. (She—Mom, not the queen—used the money you gave her to finish paying for her journalism degree, moved to America, and we lived in Los Angeles for many years while she worked as a reporter for the Times. Not the queen, Mom.)

I'm sure you get these kinds of letters all the time, so I've enclosed my DNA results, as well as most recent blood work. If you prefer your own physicians to examine me, tough nuts . . . I hate needles.

My mother passed away recently without ever telling me who you were. When her attorney read me her last will and testament, I was pretty shocked, and it's why I had to write to you.

To tell you a little about myself, I am five foot seven, with blue eyes and dark brown hair. My birthday is March 20, 1972. I enjoy tennis, cooking, and the collected works of Pat McManus and Carl Hiaasen. I work as a hunting and fishing guide for the Outer

Banks Co. out of Juneau, and in my spare time I punch up scripts for Hollywood. The former is infinitely more satisfying, but the latter pays the rent.

I don't expect to hear from you, so don't feel bad. To be blunt, I can understand how a bastard popping up out of nowhere would be awkward for you and the rest of the royals. I just wanted you to know about me, but I understand you have many responsibilities, both family and professional.

I've attached my contact information in case you want a lackey to reach me. But if I don't hear anything, no hard feelings.

Sir, I hope this letter finds you in all good health.

Sincerely yours,
Nicole

Part One

BASTARD

Chapter 1

"Holy mother of God!" King Alexander II yowled.

Jeffrey Rodinov, who had been casually leaning against the closed door of the king's office, instantly sprang back, then went through the door. He didn't open it and run through. He *went through* the door, his nine mil in his left hand. The safety was off. It was always off.

"Sir, get down!"

"I'm having a heart attack here, Rodinov, so don't point that thing at me." The king had a piece of paper crumpled in a large fist. "Holy Jesus! My God!"

Jeffrey snatched his two-way from his right hip, pressed the Call button, and barked, "Code seventeen, the Boss's office, *yesterday*." In other words, Dr. Hedman, get your ass up here pronto.

"Can you believe this? I can't friggin' believe this." The black-haired, blue-eyed king, head of the Royal House of Baranov, was normally the picture of florid health. Right now he was as pale as the paper he was clutching.

Jeffrey had never seen him like that, not even after he'd been shot four years ago. (The first, and last, vacation Jeffrey had ever taken. Left the country for one damn month and the whole place fell apart.)

"Sir," Jeffrey began, only to be interrupted as Edmund Dante, the king's majordomo, galloped through the shattered doorway, then screeched to a halt in front of the large mahogany desk.

"My king," Edmund gasped. "How may I assist you?"

It was a day for surprises; Jeffrey had never seen Mr. Dante so rattled. The king's special assistant was as tall as His Majesty, but thin as a stick. He had served the Baranovs since time out of mind and as such, had no fear of any of them.

He also had two master's degrees, one in Alaskan history, the other in Alaskan literature. The princesses had nicknamed him Ichabod Brain, something no one—not even the king—would dare say to his face.

Edmund Dante ruled the royal family with equal parts love and uncompromising ruthlessness. The RST (Royal Security Team) had as much respect for Dante as they did for any of their charges. They also took bets on whether Mr. Dante had ice water for blood or nothing at all.

"Is anyone going to tell me what's going on?" Dante asked mildly.

Jeffrey shook splinters out of his hair. "He yelled. I came. Nobody's here; it's clean. Doc's on the way."

"I don't need a damned doctor!"

Edmund stared critically at the doorway. "No, but you certainly need a carpenter. At the risk of wasting time by repeating myself, my king, how can I be of service?"

The king gargled in reply and thrust the smushed paper at his assistant. Edmund read it in four seconds, then read it again.

"Hmmm."

"That's it? Hmmm? I'll hmmm your scrawny butt, Dante."

"I tremble before your wrath, my king. May I see the envelope?"

"I thought you screened all the king's mail," Jeffrey asked, dying to know what was in the mysterious letter, but too proud to ask.

"Ninety percent," Edmund replied absently, glancing at the envelope, which had been neatly slit by one of the battalion of royal secretaries.

"Yeah, and I keep telling you to ramp it up to ninety-five," the king said, gesturing to the piles of paper all over his desk.

Mr. Dante ignored the king; he was probably the only person in the country who could get away with it. "A few things slip by. Perhaps one of the admins read it and felt it was for the king's eyes only."

"Ya think?" The king ran his blocky fingers through his thick black hair. Although in his early sixties, he looked fifteen years younger, with very little gray in the hair he had passed on to nearly all of his children. "I got another kid running around?"

"Or not." Edmund was now looking at a piece of paper that was still in the envelope. "DNA tests can be faked. This entire thing may be a fake. You have not forgotten you are the seventh richest man on the planet, I trust."

"Well, holy old cripes, I guess it slipped my mind."

"Mr. Rodinov, will you kindly holster your weapon? Goose season is several months away."

"Yes, sir." Jeffrey didn't bother to point out that a nine mil would be a poor weapon for hunting geese. "Majesty, if you don't need me, I'll be at my post."

"Thanks, Jeff." Only the king got away with that; he hated the nickname. "And thanks for the response time. Sorry I scared you. Cancel the doc, okay?"

"Quite all right, sir. And I will." Jeffrey bowed but, as Baranov royal protocol was much less rigid than most other royal protocols, was able to turn his back on the king and walk out.

He canceled the code seventeen, then took up his usual position, but since there was no longer a door, could hear everything. That was fine. That was more than fine. He liked being invisible. It made his job infinitely easier.

The Boss and Mr. Dante's voice drifted into the hallway. Jeffrey took it as a mark of trust that neither of them bothered to lower their voices. "My king, there is one question on my—"

"Yeah, you know I had doubts about marrying Dara."

"I was always surprised you went along with an arranged marriage."

"Hey, my dad was sick and it was what he wanted. And you know how it is—a crown prince without heirs makes everybody nervous. But I still felt like they were jamming that wildcat down my throat. So I had a fling before the wedding. Nice gal. Really nice gal. Bartender, like the letter said. The woman made a mean Rusty Nail and that's no lie."

"Fascinating."

"We had a good time. She knew who I was and didn't give a ripe shit. I liked that. Hell, I loved it."

"And then . . . ?"

"And then I got married. She knew the score; we had a nice good-bye and that was that. She never told me about any baby. Why didn't she tell me?"

"I'm still trying to deduce why she bedded you," Edmund admitted.

"Shaddup. Not a peep. Never asked me for a thing, never wrote me, never called. I just thought . . . you know.

A nice memory and that was it. Then Dara got knocked up right away with David and we were off to the races."

"So you're saying it is biologically possible."

"You kidding? I was barely out of my teens. I could go all night in those days. And we did, believe me."

"Majesty, could you hand me that trash can? I'm feeling the uncontrollable urge to vomit blood."

"Knock it off, tight ass. First thing we gotta do is find out if this, uh—"

"Nicole, Majesty."

"Yeah, if this Nicole is the real deal. And then—"

"Perhaps it's best if we take it one thing at a time, my king."

"Yeah, perhaps."

"I will contact the lab that did these tests. If they verify the blood work, I will make arrangements for our own tests."

"Yeah, but she says she doesn't want any more needles."

Jeffrey heard a short silence, and then a distinctive sound: Edmund snorting. "You are her king, sire, and your will is Alaska's will. Her wishes have no bearing on the situation."

"Great, Edmund. Spoken like a true Nazi."

"I live to serve, Majesty."

Chapter 2

Nicole Krenski, bastard princess of Alaska, daughter of a bartender and a king, counted to ten.

"Hey, I almost got that one," her client chirped, yanking on his fishing rod with all his might.

"That'd be great, Jim, if we were fishing for pine trees. Give that to me." *Before I stick it up your ass.* With a few practiced tugs, the Daredevil lure freed itself from the tree and plopped into the water. Nicole slowly started reeling it in, and felt a nibble. "Okay, you got a bite. Now remember what I told you." *Twenty-five times.* "Carefully set the hook and—"

He snatched the rod from her hands and gave a mighty yank, which only ripped the lure out of the fish's mouth.

"Hey, I think I'm getting the hang of this!"

Nicole scowled at the short (her height) balding stock broker on vacation from New York City. "Jimmy?"

"Yeah, babe?"

"Do not call me babe. And if you ever take a fishing rod away from me without my permission, you'll be shitting five-pound test line for three days."

Jimmy gulped and managed a smile. Nicole knew full well that clients hit on her when they got a look at her tits and eyes and whatnot, and gave up when she proved she had nothing in her veins but river water. At least as far as her customers were concerned, she'd sooner lay a grizzly than someone who paid her bills.

Jimmy sketched a mock salute. "You got it, boss lady. Ready to try again?"

"Sure." *One. Two. Three. Four. Five.* "Nice and easy. Use your wrist, not your arm." *Six. Seven. Eight.* "Release the bale. And—you've caught another tree."

Meekly, Jimmy handed back his rod. "Could you get that out of the branch for me, please?"

"My pleasure," she groaned. *Oh God, please save me from tourists. Especially big city tourists.*

"Maybe we should try a different spot."

"Maybe I should try a different client."

"That's cold, babe. I guess we really *are* in Alaska."

"You don't know what cold is. And don't call me babe."

Chapter 3

Exhausted—more from Jimmy's refusal to learn anything other than any real physical exertion—Nicole dropped him off at the Juneau branch of the Outer Banks Co. office and drove to her trailer, faking a cheerful wave as she sped off in her pick-up. At least this one hadn't tried to grab her boobs when she bent over to tie on a sinker. And when *did* that guy get out of the hospital? Her boss had told her but she'd forgotten.

As always, her spirits lifted at the sight of the neat brown and cream mobile home at the far edge of the Juneau town limits. It was small, but she didn't need much space, and the large shed held all her hunting and fishing equipment.

Best of all, the trailer backed up to 500 acres of wilderness. She'd had deer, possums, raccoons, snakes, rabbits, bears, and moose in her yard. Sparrows, woodpeckers, blue jays, hummingbirds, chickadees, plovers, and terns visited the dozen birdfeeders she kept full. And occasionally, Great Gray Owls swooped down and helped themselves to a plover or chickadee. Ah, well. Nature red in tooth and claw and all that.

Once a gut-shot deer had staggered into the yard and she'd put the poor thing out of its agony with a quick shot to the head with one of her rifles. The doe had never had a chance; it had been trailing viscera through her yard. She'd then called the Game Warden; when he showed up, he'd offered her the venison. She had declined, having a freezer full of wild game. She hoped the idiot who hadn't bothered to track his kill would contract malaria in the near future.

Nicole carefully put her equipment away, locked the shed, then went through her front door. The place was immaculate, as usual, and sparsely furnished, as she liked it. Perfect order, perfect solitude. Her CDs and books were alphabetized; all the cans and boxes in the pantry were lined up. If only her mother had—

But her mother's death was too recent and raw, and she shoved the thought away, hard. Her mother had left her enough money to buy the trailer new, for cash, and not much else. Oh, and her mother had also left her a favor. A last wish, as it were.

Her answering machine was blinking. She knew it wasn't the office; they didn't guide at night. She knew it wasn't her dead mother. She had no friends, only acquaintances, and hadn't been laid since her mother had gotten sick. Therefore . . .

Dammit.

She stabbed the Play button and heard a cultured, cool voice say, "Miss Krenski, my name is Edmund Dante and I am calling from the Sitka Palace regarding a letter you sent King Alexander. His Majesty the king requires an audience with you at once, as well as an examination by the royal physician. Please call me at 907-263-9331 at your earliest convenience. Thank you." Click.

Nicole chewed her lip and thought about it. And thought about it some more.

And then she erased the message.

Chapter 4

Nicole erased the new message the next day.
And the next.
And the next.

Chapter 5

Nicole dropped her client, a perfectly pleasant family practitioner named Sandra Dee, of all things, at the Outer Banks Co. and pocketed the generous tip.

Sandra Dee, also from New York City, had caught on at once and spent the afternoon kicking ass and filling the live well. The small redhead nearly staggered under the weight of the fish on her stringer. Nicole unhitched the boat trailer, mentally promising her boss she'd come back first thing in the morning and hose it down.

Nicole couldn't help but laugh as her giddy client bounded up the steps to the office with one final wave over her shoulder. These were the best days for her: showing someone a skill they had not known they possessed. Showing a stranger the utter and mystifying beauty of the Alaskan wilderness and recognizing the look on their face, the awe of someone at a stirring church service.

She swung by Chicken Lickin' for a three-piece meal, hold the biscuits, extra gravy. Mmm . . . gravy. She'd drink it by the glass if she could. The thought made her grin.

Her smile faded as she saw the long black car parked in her driveway and the two men loitering on her front lawn. She didn't slow and didn't look in that direction again. She stared straight ahead—*nope, nothing wrong here, and I certainly don't live there, which is why I'm not looking at you two*—and kept going past her trailer.

She found the back trail leading into the woods, got out of her truck and locked the hubs, then got back in, engaged the four-wheel drive, and bounced and jounced until she was only half a mile from the south side of her property.

Muttering under her breath, Nicole popped open her glove compartment and pulled out the .38. A poor weapon at long range, but she had every expectation of getting nice and close. Besides, the rest of her guns were in the shed. She cursed herself for not installing a gun rack in the truck. Well, maybe next week.

Nicole locked the truck (some of her rods were custom made) and stole through the forest on foot, noisy as a salamander. She came up on her trailer from behind, knelt, and carefully slid aside the panel to the left of the back door. She belly crawled beneath her trailer until she was beside her porch.

One of the men was sitting on her porch; the other one—the armed one, no mistaking the bulge on his hip, even from the road—was standing beside him. In fact, he was standing about nine inches in front of her face.

She supposed most single women might wonder why armed strangers were waiting for her in her yard, but she'd never been one to sweat the why of things.

She noiselessly slid the panel back, reached, clutched his ankles, and yanked. The man hit the ground face first and in a flash she vaulted from cover, sat on him, and pressed the barrel of her gun to the back of his head.

"That's a .38," she informed him. "Normally a pea shooter, but at this range, it'll ruin your week."

"Ow," the man said calmly into the grass.

She relieved him of his sidearm, a spotless nine millimeter, and tossed it behind her, beneath her trailer. "When you get it back, you might want to break it down and hit it with some gun oil. It's pretty dirty under there. Also, I don't like surprises."

"I never would have guessed," the stranger mumbled into the turf.

"Oh, for God's sake," the man on the porch said in a deep voice, sounding exasperated and charmed at once. She turned her head, not moving the gun.

"You!"

"Me," the King of Alaska replied agreeably. He was dressed in jeans and a blue oxford shirt with the sleeves rolled up to the elbows. He had his chin cupped in his hand (he needed a shave) and took her in at a glance: the brunette hair, the blue eyes, the dirty shirt and jeans, the gun.

"Yep," he said, sounding almost . . . cheerful? "You're one of mine, all right. Nice to meet you, Nicole."

Chapter 6

"Go away," Nicole said warmly.

"Aw, don't be like that, kiddo. And would you mind putting away the pea shooter? You're hurting Jeff's feelings."

"Not to mention my kidneys," the man mumbled into the ground.

She carefully got off the man but kept the gun at her side.

"That's better," the king said as Jeff climbed slowly to his feet. "So, I'm Al, your dad. And we know who you are. That's Jeff, head of my detail."

She smirked. "And you're not dead yet?" She was being nasty because she was so completely distracted by the bodyguard's size. When he stood, he went up and up and up. Well over six feet and probably 220, none of it fat. He was built like a linebacker. He hadn't looked so big from the road. Or so gorgeous.

No. She did not think that. Sure, he had lush, curly black hair—true black, not dark brown—and pale blue eyes. Sniper's eyes. He had a built-in tan (was he part Akiak? or maybe Ekok?) and the muscular definition of a champion lifter. His head and hands were blocky, like they had been carved by a skilled craftsman who was in a hurry. He filled out his black tailored suit—a man his size couldn't buy off the rack—superbly.

Gorgeous? Please. She was just distracted because she hadn't been laid in 29 months and 18 days.

"Sire," he was saying, "I apologize. I will tender my resignation at—"

"The hell. I didn't hear a thing either. Serves us right for showing up on her turf without calling. Oh, wait. Edmund's been leaving her messages all week." The king beamed at her. "Should have had the palace guards drag you to my place instead."

"Dead palace guards," she informed him. "Mutilated subjects. Body parts all over the Sitka Palace."

"I see you inherited none of your mother's charm. Just my mouth. Oh, and my fabulous good looks," he added modestly.

"Like you knew a thing about my mother." It made her angry, it *enraged* her, to hear this pampered cheating bastard talk about her dear dead mom. "She was a fling, a one-night stand that lasted for a week or two."

"She was lovely and sweet and funny, and you will *watch your tone* when you speak to me, Nicole."

She almost took a step backward. He hadn't been smiling. He hadn't been fucking around. He had sounded like—well, like a king.

"Sorry," she muttered.

The king cheered up instantly. "That's all right. It's been a weird week for everybody. So if you'll just hop in the car, we can go back to the palace and—"

"No."

"What?"

"No, King Alexander."

"Bad idea," Jeff said quietly at her left shoulder.

Without turning her head, she snarled, "Nobody hit your buzzer, Jeff."

"*Please* don't call me Jeff," he whispered in her ear. Annoyingly, all the hairs on her left arm stiffened to attention, and she jerked her head away from his mouth.

The king coughed. "Uh, Nicole, I'm sorry we got off on the wrong foot, but I wasn't exactly asking."

"I'm not going and I do not submit to your authority, sir."

"Uh." The king shot Jeff a look and coughed again. "You sort of don't have a—"

"How quickly we forget, King Cheats-on-His-Fiancée. You might want to reread my letter. My mother and father were Alaskan citizens, but I was born in Los Angeles."

The king scowled. "Dual citizenship."

"Right-o." Under Alaskan law, merely residing in Alaska did not mean you were a subject of the king. You needed to be Alaskan on both sides and born in the country. Any deviation resulted in dual citizenship, and the gentleman (or bastard princess) in question could claim the other country as her own. "So thanks for stopping by, ta-ta, so long, get lost."

The king stood and, like Jeff, he went up and up and up. Of course, he was standing two steps above her, but still. She craned her head to glare up at him. "Go away now."

"I don't get it," he complained.

"I'm not surprised. Mom didn't like you for your keen intellect."

The bodyguard actually flinched, but the king didn't move. Instead, he scowled down at her. "I'm gonna let that one go by."

"Thanks gobs."

His black brows caromed together and his eyes were dark blue slits. But she would not be intimidated! Well, not much.

"If you didn't want to see me," he bitched, "and you don't want to come to the palace, why the hell did you write me that letter?"

"Because my mother asked me to. It was in her will. She told me about you and she asked me to get in touch, and that was *all* she asked." And it was damn sure all she was going to do. "It was the only thing she ever asked of me in twenty years."

"Oh." Then, quietly, "I'm sorry about your mother. She was wonderful."

Tears stung her eyes; on the whole, she preferred him kingly and commanding and generally acting like a jerk. "Go," she said. "Please."

The bodyguard—Jeff—reached under her trailer with a long arm and retrieved his gun. He gave her a look she couldn't figure as the king thumped down her steps.

"Well," the king said after an awkward pause.

"Good-bye," she said.

Without another word, they left.

Nicole fumbled for her door, ran into the trailer, collapsed on the couch, and wept for fifteen minutes. Then she got up, walked to the bathroom, washed her face, and kicked a hole in the cupboard under the sink.

Chapter 7

Alexander Baranov, descendant of Russian rebels who took a country for themselves, bounded into his office, with Jeff right on his heels. Edmund was spreading out various paperwork for him to sign, which on any other occasion would have dampened his mood and made him contemplate loading a shotgun.

"Good heavens," Edmund said, eyeing the rumpled Jeff. For Edmund, that was the equivalent of "Holy hell!" "What happened to you, Jeffrey?"

"My kid," Al couldn't help bragging. "She got the drop on both of us."

Edmund blinked slowly, like a gecko. This was the equivalent of anyone else yelling, "Oh my God!"

"My king, I remind you that we have yet to verify our own DNA testing and—"

"Yeah, yeah, but I'm telling you. She's the spitting image of Alex and Kathryn. She's got the Baranov blue eyes and the dark hair." Al plopped into his chair as Jeff took up his position just inside the doorway. Al knew Jeff's humiliation was a live thing, a stinging thing, and he would stay closer than usual until the sting wore off. Although he was pleased with Nicole, he felt for his proud bodyguard and made no comment when Jeff didn't leave the office.

"Mouthy, too," Al continued, trying not to grin and failing. "I didn't see much of her mother in her, to tell the truth. But I know it like I know how to gut a salmon: Nicole Krenski is my daughter."

"Pure poetry as usual, my king. May I meet her?"

"Uh." Al glanced at Jeff, who remained a stone. "Well, she refused to come with us."

Edmund, tidying still more paperwork, froze. This was the equivalent of anyone else yelling, "What the holy hell are you talking about?!?"

After a long silence, Edmund straightened and put his fingers together, Mr. Burns style. The only thing missing was a drawn-out "Ehhhxxxceleeent."

Edmund took a breath and let it out. "She . . . refused?"

"Flat out."

"But she cannot. She may be royalty, but she is also your subject, and as such, she—"

"Nope, dual citizenship."

"Dual . . . ah." Edmund tapped his long, skinny fingers together. "But if she refused to return with you, then why did she bother to—ah. Perhaps her mother asked her to? A, erm, dying wish, perhaps?"

"Right on the nose, Eddie."

"Sire, if you call me that again I shall instantly tender my resignation, and then disembowel you."

"He threatened the king," Al told Jeff. "That's worth prison time. My great granddaddy signed the bill himself."

Jeff didn't move, or speak. It was the rare week Edmund didn't threaten to resign or slaughter the royal family, or both.

"God, what a kid," Al continued, leaning back in his

chair and lacing his fingers behind his head. He sighed happily. "Got the drop on us, jammed that .38 in the back of Jeff's head—"

There was the dull thud as Jeff banged the back of his head on the wall, his eyes closed. Politely, Al and Edmund ignored it.

"—sassed me like you wouldn't believe, then kicked us off her property. It was unbelievably wonderful."

"It, er, sounds unbelievably wonderful."

Jeffrey banged his head again.

With a worried glance at the head of his detail, the king finished, "Nobody's talked to me like that since Christina joined the family."

"She certainly sounds like a Baranov," Edmund admitted. "Sire, it is vital we verify her bloodline. You realize the ramifications."

Al did. He wondered what his eldest son, David, would think about all this. What all the kids would think.

"D'you think I should tell the kids now or wait until we have proof?"

Edmund hesitated. "My king, I would not presume to advise you on such a personal matter."

Jeffrey made a strangled sound that he managed to turn into a cough; Al laughed outright. "Since when? You got a fever or something, Edmund?"

Jeff cleared his throat. It sounded like gravel in a blender. "Let me go back, Majesty."

Surprised, Al glanced at his bodyguard. "What? Jeff? Did you hit your head too hard on the wall?"

"Sire, let me go back and try again."

"Jeez, I dunno . . . I thought we'd give her a little space before trying again."

"My king, you know that is unacceptable!" Edmund was

as upset as Al had ever seen, and that was saying something. He had actually raised his voice. “We cannot let this sleeping dog lie!”

“Try to resist referring to my kid as a dog.”

“I require proof she *is* your kid, my king. And you know why. And you know we cannot delay.”

The king shifted uncomfortably in his chair. “Yeah, but—”

“Sire, forgive the interruption, but let me go back,” Jeff urged. “First thing tomorrow. I’ll switch detail with Reynolds. I can do this. Please let me do this.”

“Jeez, Jeff . . .”

“With all do respect, Jeffrey, if the king could not persuade her, I fail to see what—”

“Hush up, Edmund. Give me a second here.”

Al thought about it. The two men let him. Finally, he said, “I don’t see the harm. And if you’re willing, it’s fine by me, Jeff.”

“Thank you, sire.”

“Wait.” This time Edmund was thinking, and the two others let him. After a short silence, Edmund made a suggestion, showing his usual cool good sense, and Al instantly accepted the advice. Then he gave Jeff his instructions.

“My king,” Jeff acknowledged, and bowed. Then he did something Al had never seen him do: he grinned.

Chapter 8

Gulping the last of her coffee, Nicole swung into the driveway of the Outer Banks Co. She was surprised to see a strange car beside her boss's and the other guides'. She nearly always beat the clients in. Who'd bother showing up at 6:30 A.M. if they didn't have to?

She hopped out of her truck, locked it, then crossed the damp lawn, enjoying the spring sunshine. Winter had a pretty good grip every year, but it always eased up, and she was always surprised when it happened. It was finally jacket weather, which meant in hot southern places like North Dakota it was shorts weather.

Spirits high, Nicole bounded up the steps and into her boss's office.

And groaned.

"We meet again, Nicole," the bodyguard told her. He was decked out for fishing—old jeans, faded flannel shirt, work boots. His curly black hair was rumpled, as if he'd spent the time waiting for her running his fingers through it. She wanted to run her fingers through it, to see if the texture was as silky as it looked.

No, she did *not.*

"Nicole, this is Jeffrey Rodinov—"

"We've met," she said shortly.

"Who works at the Sitka Palace," her boss, Mike Freeborg, continued excitedly. A Minnesotan who had moved to Juneau fourteen years ago, Mike looked quite a bit like his Norwegian forebearers: large, broad-shouldered, blond hair, green eyes. The other guides called him The Viking. And although he looked fierce, he had the temperament of a pampered kitten. "And he asked for you personally."

Nicole groaned again.

"You okay?"

"No."

"Diarrhea?"

"I wish."

"Oh." Mike shrugged his massive shoulders. "Well, anyway, show him a good time."

"I will *not*." She felt her face getting hot, which made her mad, which made her redder.

Oblivious, Mike continued. "Fill the boat—not that you're taking the boat—so he goes back to the palace and tells them all about our little outfit here."

"I quit," Nicole said.

"You can't quit," her boss yawned, showing his back fillings. Nicole quit three or four times a month. "Sandra Dee's coming back next month and she also asked for you personally. That was a five-hundred-dollar tip, right?"

"Then I'm on vacation effective this minute."

"Ha! We both know you have no life at all. This job *is* your vacation."

She cursed his perfect estimation of her character.

"Now get going."

Nicole glared at the bodyguard, who smiled back. "Prepare for a day in the darkest depths of hell," she informed him.

"Oh, I'm prepared," he replied. "I'm bristling with weapons and pepper spray, not to mention my rape whistle." Courteously, he opened the door for her. "After you, Nicole."

Chapter 9

Jeffrey landed the fish, deftly worked the hook out of its lower lip, and then tossed it back into the river.

Nicole was sitting beside him on the bank, her head in her hands. "You know how to fish," she mumbled into her palms.

"Could be I went out a time or two with my dad," he admitted, baiting the hook and casting again.

"And you sound like a local."

"As local as you can get," he admitted. "Russian on my dad's side, Ekok on my mom's."

"That explains the blue eyes and the built-in tan. You're sure as hell not a tourist. You don't need me to take you out."

"Maybe I haven't been able to get you out of my mind since you shoved your gun into my head." This, unfortunately, was nothing but the truth.

Nicole jerked her head up and glared at him. He froze, mesmerized by the Baranov blue eyes. Funny how he knew six other people with eyes that exact same shade, none of which had the same effect on him. "Very funny. You can go back and tell the king he'll die of old age before I show up and get poked and prodded, and then play princess for him and those other weirdos."

"Those other weirdos," he said mildly, "are your family."

"Maybe I'm lying. Maybe it's a hoax."

He laughed.

She jumped up and stomped her foot. "You don't ***know.*** So don't pretend blue eyes and dark hair is a ticket into the royal family. *You've* got blue eyes and dark hair."

He yawned. "My family has been taking care of the royals for three generations. I know a Baranov when I see one. And so does the king."

"The king," she muttered, pacing back and forth on the bank. She cursed as she stepped into some mud, shook her foot, then nearly overbalanced into the river, and cursed more. Jeffrey listened with admiration; she knew swear words he didn't, and he'd done a stretch in the AAF (Alaskan Air Force). "Did he tell you he cheated on his fiancée with my mom, and then *dumped* her to get married?"

"Lucky for you," he pointed out.

She actually gurgled with rage and her hands snapped into fists. He faked a cough so she wouldn't see him grin or hear him laugh.

"Do you always do that?" she demanded.

"What?"

"Make unanswerable observations?"

"Only with you."

"Oh, how romantic," she mocked, fluttering her long black lashes. "It gets me right here."

He certainly hoped so. Because she was really something. Gorgeous, mouthy, smart, knew her way around a fishing pole. Killer body . . . slim, but muscular; doing guide work kept her in good shape. Trim-hipped in blue jeans, a red T-shirt, and a bright blue windbreaker; the spring breeze had kissed roses into her cheeks and made her eyes sparkle. Or perhaps glitter with rage; it was hard to tell.

Jeffrey tried to understand why this particular Baranov had such an effect on him. He certainly hadn't been attracted to Kathryn or Alex. Of course, he'd known them since they were kids. And God knew he wasn't attracted to the king, or the other Alex. Of course, he wasn't gay or bi. So why this one?

Because Nicole was different. She had royal blood in her veins but was raised by a commoner. The two of them against the world, no doubt. He doubted she had the slightest idea of the effect she had on men. Those magnetic blue eyes alone—

He felt a nibble, waited with the patience of a python, and then at a firmer bite set the hook and reeled it in, unhooked it, tossed it back into the river with a plop, and then baited his hook again.

"Plus you're doing catch and release! You don't even need me to clean them for you. There's no reason for me to be here at all."

"There's every reason."

"Oh, please, can we stop with the Obi-Wan speak? What's your game plan, slick?"

"To charm you into coming back to the palace with me."

"Ha!"

"Why not? You had to know this would happen when you wrote what you wrote."

"When I wrote what I wrote?" She stopped pacing and stared down at him. "You didn't read it?"

"Of course not. And I would never ask. It was the king's personal correspondence."

"Oh. Uh, I didn't think about it that way. That you didn't—sorry," she said, looking like the apology tasted bad.

Again, he had to force a cough. "Well, I wrote him who I was, reminded him about my mom, left my phone number, and that was about it."

"Well, as I said, you had to know there would be consequences."

"It's not like I had a choice, did I?"

"Your mother's dying wish?"

"Now how did you know *that?*"

"Edmund Dante guessed, and the king confirmed. Mr. Dante is the man who has been leaving messages for you. He pretty much runs the palace, and the royal family."

"Swell. He tries to run me and I'll break both his ankles."

"Tough to do from a riverbank."

"Oh no you don't! I'm wise to you, Mr. Bodyguard."

Oh no you aren't, sweetie.

"I have another bite," he said smugly.

"And I," she announced, "have a migraine."

Chapter 10

Well! She handled yesterday pretty well, considering. Considering the fact that she wondered what he looked like with his shirt off.

No, she did *not.*

Oh yes, you did, liar. Can't you be honest with yourself ever?

"Shut up," she snapped at herself. She occasionally had entire conversations with herself. Most of the time she attempted to keep them inside her brain.

But! She had handled him just fine. Refused to head back to the, God forbid, Sitka Palace. Sent him on his merry way. Ignored Freeborg's insistence she give him a blow-by-blow recap. Drove home. Had McNuggets. Didn't think about him once.

Liar!

"Shut up!" she yowled, slamming on her brakes and wincing at what the spraying gravel was doing to her truck's ruby red paint job. She shut it off, shoved the door open, fairly leaped to the ground, and then darted into the office.

And groaned.

"Nicole!" Freeborg yodeled when he saw her. "He's back! And he brought—"

"I know who the crown prince is, Mike, Gawd." She ignored Prince David Baranov's outstretched hand and scowled. "Everybody who reads *People* or *The Juneau Empire* knows who he is. Got an overwhelming urge to fish, Prince David? Not enough protein up at the palace?"

"Actually, I need some food for my penguins, but that's not why I'm here."

"Well, don't let the door hit you between the eyes on your way out."

By reply, the prince turned to Jeffrey and said, "Uh-huh. I see what you mean."

"Talk about me like I'm not here again and you'll be a neutered crown prince. And then where would we be?"

"Nicole!" her boss screamed, horrified.

Prince David grinned and pointed a finger at her. "Jailable offense! Maybe a month or two behind bars will make the palace look like a better option."

"Try it."

"Uh, Your Highness, she tends to go about heavily armed." Jeffrey was nervously eyeing her windbreaker.

"What, 'heavily'? It was a lousy .38."

"Did you really get the drop on him? Dad said it, but it was still kind of hard to believe." David jerked a thumb over his shoulder at Jeffrey. His eyes, the same shade as hers, twinkled at her. She wondered if he could make them do that on purpose. "He's kind of got a reputation, y'know."

"Uh—what's going on?" her boss asked, the color leaking back into his face. He was glancing from her to the prince and back again. "Do you know His Highness?"

"No."

"But I know her," Prince David said cheerfully. "Only by reputation, of course. So, what is it? Why won't you come back? Hate needles? Doctor-o-phobic?"

"Iatrophobia," she corrected him. "And no."

"Uh-huh. You know a word I've never heard before—and

I'm a PhD," he added modestly. "But noooo, you're not scared."

"Of course I'm scared. Do you have any idea how *weird* you all are? Your brother Nicholas was in all the papers—again—for pulling that prank that cost Prince Henry a broken ankle!"

David winced. "Don't remind me. Dad took a ration of shit from the Queen of England for that one. Don't sweat it, though. Nicky's safely confined to the palace until his twenty-fifth birthday."

"What a relief for the planet. And the Windsors."

"Oh, like Henry wasn't in on the whole—"

"Look, my mom asked me to do something. I did it. It's done. We're. All. Done. Now, buh-bye."

"But you're supposed to take me salmon fishing," the prince whined.

"According to some, I'm supposed to do a lot of things."

Her boss was banging his blond head on his blond-wood desk. "Nicole, you're killing me. Please stop. I'm begging. I'm groveling. I'm—"

"No worries, Mr. Freeborg. I promise your business won't be penalized as a result of anything my sister says."

The blond head jerked up. Nicole closed her eyes. "Your *what*?"

"Well." Nicole opened her eyes in time to see the Crown Prince of Alaska wink at her. "Half sister."

Chapter 11

David Baranov, Crown Prince of Alaska, plopped down in the chair in front of the king's desk. Relieved to have a break from reading tedious legislation, Al all but shoved the paperwork away from him. "Come in! Sit down! Spend some time with your old man."

"Dad, you've got to finish that stuff up sooner or later."

"Shut up, you."

"It's a wonder anything gets done. If you're not stalling, you're sneaking out to go fishing."

"Put your mouth in Park, boy."

His son mimed locking his lips shut, then tossed an imaginary key over his shoulder.

"Well?"

David shook his head. "No go, Dad. And for the record, no one has ever spoken to me like that in my life. Except for you. And . . . well. Is it just me, or does she remind me of Christina?"

"She reminds me of every one of you brats," the king growled.

"Yeah, the resemblance was hard to miss. And not just on the physical side." David paused. "Have you, ah, told the other sibs about this yet?"

"No."

"Oh." Pause. Al fought the urge to roll his eyes. *Here comes the moral assurance that I haven't gone down in his estimation.* "Listen, Dad. I had all last night and all day today to think about it. And I don't—I mean, I know you and Mom weren't exactly thrilled with each other a hundred percent of the time, and I'm sure Nicole's mother was what you needed at just the right time. I just, you know. Understand."

"What a relief. I love you, boy, but I require neither your permission nor your assurance."

"*Sieg heil*, Your Majesty."

His eldest son stretched out long legs and yawned. He had the distinct air of fish guts about him and was dressed casually. Al was always startled to see how much his boy looked exactly like a younger version of him. It was like looking into a sneaky mirror.

Hell, it didn't seem so long since he'd been David's age. Objectively, it had been decades. Subjectively, it felt like maybe five years. Hell, he was a father by the time he was David's age.

Of course, David was a father now, too. The king smiled, thinking of his granddaughter, Dara.

"Oh, and she's only the best angler I've ever seen," his son teased, bringing Al back to the conversation.

"Second best," the king grumped. "And don't you forget it, boy. You're not too big to spank."

"Actually, I really sort of am. Think of how Dara would be scarred to see her grandfather assaulting her father! She could be the Queen of Alaska someday, and yet psychologically crippled."

"Meh." So, he mused. David had obviously gone fishing. Nicole had agreed to take him out, as she'd taken Jeffrey out. Maybe there was a way to crack this egg yet. "You get anything else out of her?"

"Yeah, she knows the technical term for an uncontrollable fear of doctors."

"Who doesn't?" he bluffed.

"Iatrophobia," his son kindly supplied.

"If that kid's scared of anything, I'll eat sushi."

"Please, Dad," his son mock-begged. "Don't befoul your gourmet palate. Hamburgers will never taste the same."

"I got to take shit from every one of my kids. Every one."

"It's your curse," his son agreed happily.

"Iatrophobia," Al mused.

"I don't think it's that simple. In fact, I think it was a feint."

"A faint?"

"She's trying to throw us off the trail. Which is exceedingly weird. She writes us about her, when she could have clammed up, and then refuses to cooperate."

"You could refuse my dying wish so easily?"

His son colored, but doggedly continued. "Who wouldn't want to be one of us? She passes the DNA, she's got a claim to one of the biggest fortunes on the planet. She'll never have to worry about money again, nor any of her kids, or grandkids. Plus, we have a pretty good time around here." David spread his palms. "What's not to love?"

Al smiled at his son. David was young. And he thought his family's way was the only way. Although Al strongly suspected his son was quite a bit more intelligent than he was, he lacked experience. Al had been walking around on the planet long enough to know just how much people feared change.

David, born and reared a prince, could not conceive of any other lifestyle, nor understand why a stranger would turn it down.

"It was her and her mama for her whole life," Al said. "And now she's all alone. Maybe she likes her solitude." Except scratch the maybe.

There was a discreet rap on the door. "C'mon in, Edmund!" they called in unison.

"Majesty. Highness." Edmund fairly staggered under the load of paperwork. Al made a conscious effort not to cringe. "May I presume to ask how it went, Your Highness?"

"Do you *see* her anywhere, Edmund?"

"Watch the tone, boy," the king said absently, drumming his fingers on the desk. One thing he had insisted on before any of his children could walk: hired help were also subjects, and subjects deserved respect. Always. Except, of course, for one. And he'd straightened *her* out, by God. Sent her packing with a flea in her ear. Again.

"Sorry, Edmund," David was saying. "My morning was equal parts aggravating and amusing. Didn't mean to mouth off."

"I know not to what you refer, Highness. Will you permit me a suggestion?"

"Don't you hate when he pretends he doesn't control our every move?"

"With all my black heart," Al replied. "Spill, Edmund."

"I think the time for gentler tactics have passed."

"You don't mean?" the prince gasped.

"The big guns?" the king guessed.

"Exactly." Edmund paused a beat. "Princess Christina."

"Dear God," king and prince said in unison.

Chapter 12

"So!" the Crown Princess of Alaska greeted her as she entered the office. "You're the numbnut who won't submit to a blood test." She stuck out an unmanicured hand. Startled, Nicole shook it. "Nice to meet you. I'm Christina."

"Uh, yeah. I read about your wedding in *People*. And your daughter's birth in—"

"*News of the Weird?*" the princess guessed.

Nicole's hand shot up, too late.

"My God," Jeffrey-the-annoying gasped. "Was that . . . a *smile*?"

"Shhhh, Jeff. Don't scare her off."

"Jeff-*rey*, Your Highness. As we've discussed, only His Majesty—"

She spun on him and said, "We've been over this a zillion times. You call me Christina, I'll call you Jeff-*rey*."

"Your Highness—"

"Yes, *Jeff?*"

"He can't," Nicole interrupted, smiling again and praying neither of them would comment. "Generations of duty to the royal family. Familiarity is beaten out of them at an early age."

"Well, screw," the princess muttered.

"*I'll* call you Christina. I'll also call you 'see you later' and 'thanks for stopping by.' "

"They said you were never at a loss for words," the perfectly cool, tall, blond woman said. Like every royal she had met so far, she was dressed casually: tan shorts (a bold move in forty-five-degree weather), a T-shirt (another bold move) with the logo I'M THE PRINCESS OF ALASKA, WHO THE HELL ARE YOU?, and a buttercup yellow sweater knotted around her waist. "They also said you looked *extraordinarily* like Alex and Kathryn, and that's true, too."

"Super duper. Well, what's up? Salmon fishing? Hiking? There's not much in season if hunting's your thing . . ."

"No, thanks. Uh, could you cool out your boss a little? He looks about ten seconds from a stroke."

Nicole was embarrassed; she'd been so distracted by Jeffrey (who was in his black tailored suit; duh, she should have known this one wasn't going fishing) and the Crown Pr—Christina that she hadn't even noticed Freeborg was at his desk.

And Christina was right. He was as pale as the belly of a trout.

"Mike? Mike!" She waved a hand in front of his glazed eyes. "It's okay. I'm not in any trouble."

"You're one of them," he accused, pointing a trembling, banana-sized finger at Christina. "Her husband said! Yesterday!"

"Oh, no," Nicole assured him, but she was looking at Jeffrey as she said it. "Not *ever*."

"Blood will tell, honey."

Then, in unison, she and Christina said, "Don't call me honey."

Alone, Christina added, "See, see? Your reputation precedes you!"

"Is that so?"

"Yup."

"And you think I'm an in-law."

"Don't think. Know."

"So, if you were trying to talk one of *them* into something they absolutely did not want to do, how do you think it would go?"

Christina opened her mouth. Then closed it. Then opened it again, looking remarkably salmon-like. Then she glared. "Don't confuse me with facts."

"That's a valid warning," Jeff added.

"Pipe down, Jeff-*rey*. One thing I've learned living with some of the richest people in the world is that everyone has a price. So what's yours?"

"What?"

"What's it gonna cost to get you to come with me and submit to our DNA test?"

"Are you implying that you can *pay* me?" *To turn my back on my mother and everything she ever did for me?* God! They were all the same! "You *bitch*!" Then she socked her. Almost. Jeffrey moved like lightning, so she actually socked him in the throat (she'd been aiming for Christina's left eye).

"Hey!" Christina yelled as Nicole's boss clawed for his wastebasket and started retching. "Rule number one: Nobody roughs up the help!"

Then Nicole saw black stars explode as Christina socked her back.

Chapter 13

"Ow ow OW!" Nicole yelled, regaining consciousness. She opened her eyes, then groaned in equal parts pain and horror. About a hundred people were crouching over her.

"—didn't mean for her to hit her head!"

"Christina, for Christ's sake. We sent you to be a diplomat—ever heard of the word?"

"Ma'am," a paramedic said, ripping the blood pressure cuff off Nicole's arm, "can you tell me where you are?"

"The seventh circle of hell," Nicole answered.

Christina elbowed two other Baranovs out of the way and peered down anxiously. "I'm so sorry, Nicole. I only meant to give you a black eye."

"*That's* an apology?" the crown prince demanded.

"I didn't mean for you to hit your head on the boss's desk when you fell!"

"How—how did you all get here so fast?" She was looking around, and in addition to two paramedics, she recognized Princess Kathryn, Prince Nicholas, Crown Prince David, Prince Alexander, Princess Alexandria, King Alexander, and her brand-new nemesis, Christina. "Does the palace have a teleporter pad?"

"You've been out cold for twenty minutes," Prince Alexander, a shorter, younger version of his brother David, told her. "We had tons of time to get here. I'm Alexander, by the way."

She clapped a hand over her eyes. "I know who you are. I know who you *all* are." Her head was on the firmest pillow ever. Who knew Freeborg kept—

"Are you okay, kiddo?" the king asked anxiously. "How many fingers am I holding up?"

"How many fingers am *I* holding up?"

"Now that's rude," Prince Alexandria said approvingly.

"*All* of you back off and give her some air," Jeffrey ordered from—ulp—directly above her. She realized with equal parts heat and cold that the pillow was him, and her head was in his lap.

As one, the royal family took three steps back.

"Your vitals are fine," the other paramedic was telling her, "but with such a long loss of consciousness I think we should run her to the hos—"

"No hospital. No doctors. No way."

"Ma'am—"

"I'll sign the NMA."

"NMA?" she heard the youngest, sixteen-year-old Nicholas, whisper to his sister Kathryn.

"No Medical Attention," Kathryn replied. "Means if she falls down the stairs and breaks both legs while barfing up blood, she can't sue."

Nicole almost laughed at the mental image, but managed to mask it as a groan of pain as she sat up.

"If you come to the hospital, you could get a prescription . . ." one of the paramedics wheedled.

"First someone tries to bribe me with money, now Vicodin? Do I have 'weak loser' written on my forehead?"

"Christina Baranov!" the king roared.

To Nicole's vast enjoyment, Christina backed away from the red-faced king so fast she nearly tripped and went sprawling. "I didn't try to bribe her with money! I just said everyone had their price!"

"Oh, I can see how that wasn't offensive," Prince Alexander snarked.

"Shut the *hell* up, Alex. I meant like how I got the run of the kitchens when I got here. I just thought maybe she'd like her own lake or something."

"A fine plan," Alexandria observed, squinting down at Nicole. "Good job, Christina. Really. Hey, Dad, let's put her in charge of defusing the situation in China."

"Hand it over," Nicole told the paramedics, who were packing up.

"What?"

"The blood you stole while I was conked."

The paramedics looked at each other with superbly faked expressions of confusion. "Blood we—"

"Nicole!"

"Stop yelling, it hurts my head!" she yelled back.

Half the light was blotted out when the king pointed a finger at her. "The Baranovs *do not steal.* Apologize at once."

"I'm so sorry," she said sweetly, "that you're sensitive about being called thieves after your ancestors stole the country from its rightful owner, Mother Russia."

There was a long, awful silence broken by Nicholas saying, "Screw the blood test. *I'm* convinced."

"If she doesn't have a legitimate DNA test supervised by our own docs in the palace, Edmund will murder us all in our beds," David explained to his siblings.

"Hold your breath waiting for *that* to happen."

"Which part?" Kathryn asked.

"Will you all keep it down?" Jeffrey rumbled from behind her. He was still sitting behind her, like she might (ha!) get dizzy and fall back in his lap again. "You're upsetting her."

"She punched you in the larynx, Jeff."

"Is *that* why he sounds so dreadful?" Kathryn whispered to her brother Alexander.

David knelt beside her, and when he spoke, it was with so much sympathy she could hardly bear it. "It *will* happen, Nicole. It has to. See, if you're really a Baranov, which everyone in this room knows you are, that means you're first in line for the throne."

"But—but you and Christina Quickknuckles are the crown prince and—"

"Nicole, you're older. Think about it."

She did. Then she crawled to her boss's wastebasket and threw up.

Chapter 14

"Oh dear," Edmund said.

"Then she hit her head and got knocked out."

"Oh."

"For twenty minutes."

"Uhm."

"And wouldn't go to the hospital."

"Naturally."

"Then David laid it out for her."

"'Laid it out'?"

"Don't play dumb."

"Oh, never, my king. But at times it seems to me you have your own code. And I left my secret royal decoder ring in my other pants."

"You know, how she's now first in line for the throne." Alaska was famous for doing it by birth order, not sex.

"Ah."

"Then she barfed."

"A reaction I myself have nearly every week."

"Then Jeff kicked us all out. I think in his heart she's one of us, so he thinks he's her bodyguard," the king said approvingly. It was early that afternoon, and the king was enjoying a beer. Edmund drank coffee and played with the oft-neglected paperwork.

"Oh, is that what he thinks?"

"Sure. Then Jeff took her home and we all came back here. I think Christina's still sulking in her suite."

"Majesty, is there a question of lawsuit against—"

"No, because Nicole threw the first punch."

"Very well."

"Of course," the king mused, taking a swig of Bud, "that might be leverage. You know, 'cooperate or we'll tell the world you tried to coldcock the crown princess.' I get the feeling she'd hate publicity."

"My king, you have read none of the newspapers I so carefully laid out for you."

"Yes, I have."

"No," Edmund said, holding up that morning's edition of *The Juneau Empire*. "You haven't."

BASTARD PRINCESS FOUND WORKING FOR OUTER BANKS CO.

Sitka Palace denies comment.

The king hurriedly drained his beer. "Oh, fuck me," he groaned.

"With regret, I do decline."

"I'm gonna barf."

"Then it must be Thursday. And, my king, you have yet one more worry."

"Nothing can be worse than this."

"Think hard," Edmund advised.

"I'm in no mood for riddles, Edmund, so just—"

His office door was slammed open and his arch enemy, Holly Bragon ("rhymes with dragon"), stood framed in the doorway. She waved that day's newspaper at him and crowed, "Bastard Princess! I fucking love it!"

"Get me another beer," he said. "Get me a six pack. Get me three six packs." Then, to the Dragon, "I fired your ass last week."

"Oh, I know, King Grumpy. But I'm baaaaack!"

Chapter 15

Edmund was still smiling as he drove to his family's summer home fifty miles outside Juneau. His duty was a never-ending joy . . . especially on days like today.

The story of the fistfight had been amazing enough. Really, the entire Krenski/Baranov saga had been amazing enough. But the look on the king's face when Miss Holly made her ill-timed return was worth a whole month of "Eddies."

Off-duty, as he was now, he normally stayed in his rooms at the palace. But spring was here, and it was time to do his annual check on his grandfather's home to get it ready for summer.

Not that he made much use of it himself, but his dear sister would require it for much of the summer, and he wanted it in tip-top shape for her.

She would also be a frequent guest at the palace, where all the children were fond of her. (*Must stop thinking of them as children*, a voice in the back of his brain whispered for the hundredth time. *His Highness the Crown Prince is thirty-four!*)

A lovely, charming woman in her fifties with Down syndrome, Edmund's sister greeted the annual house's opening with the unbridled delight of a precocious child.

He would die for her. And if she understood death,

Geraldine would have died for him. Since he expected to precede her in death by some time (she had been a late-in-life baby for his parents, a true Lost Boy who had never grown up), he had made generous arrangements for her care as long as she lived.

And if he hadn't been able to do this thing, the king, with typical generosity (while claiming to be heartless and indifferent), had assured him many times that Geraldine would never have to worry about paying bills or cooking meals.

No matter when he passed on (hopefully via a brain aneurysm while scolding one of his beloved Baranovs), Geraldine would want for nothing.

To his surprise, as he drove up the long, tree-lined driveway, he saw another parked car. He hit the high beams and saw someone waiting for him on the wrap-around porch. In all his years of service, that had never happened.

His chest tightened; he prayed nothing had gone seriously wrong at the palace. *Please no one is sick or hurt. Please no one is sick or hurt. Please no one—*

He nearly leaped out of his car and ran to the porch—not much fun at his age—and his heart rate slowed dramatically when he saw who it was.

"Good evening, Miss Krenski," he tried not to gasp. "I trust you are well."

Chin in her hand, she squinted up at him. "You okay, slick? You're not gonna keel over on me, are you?"

"Hopefully not."

"How'd you know who I was?"

"Who else *could* you be?" he said warmly. "And it grieves me to point out you have not answered me. Are you quite well, Miss Krenski? No ill effects after this afternoon's, ah, misunderstanding?"

"Well, I've had a bitch of a headache all damn day, and the next time I see the crown princess it is awwwwn. Oh, and I'm gonna be the next fucking Queen of fucking Alaska. Other than that, I'm *great.*"

After decades of practice, Edmund had the best poker face on the planet. *O, my king, you were so right. She is of your blood.* "I see. Please, come in. I'm afraid I can offer you nothing in the way of refreshments—"

"I know. This is your family's summer home. You just came up to check it out."

"And how did you know that?" he asked, holding the door for royalty as he had done thousands, no millions of times before.

"Vee haff ways," she said, and grinned at him. His heart did a little flip-flop in his chest, and he realized anew what the king and the new princess did not: Jeffrey Rodinov was *not* sticking close because he wanted to be her bodyguard.

"I brought take-out," she said absently, preceding him. "Heard you get weak in the knees at the thought of bad Chinese food."

"We all have our vices," he admitted, and closed the door.

Chapter 16

"So lay it out for me, Mr. Dante," Nicole said to the tall, neatly dressed, skinny guy she pegged to be in his early seventies. Guy moved like a matador, though, and she guessed that running around after the royals kept him in good shape. And he sure got over a surprise in a hurry. Another occupational hazard. "Let's say I lose my tiny mind and go to the palace tomorrow and get this damn DNA test. What happens then?"

"Assuming it's positive—"

"It'll be positive," she said glumly, poking at her beef and broccoli with a chopstick. "Unless this is my mom's idea of a disgusting practical joke."

He spooned more rice onto his plate. "Your status will be confirmed to the press. Arrangements will be made for you to move into the palace. Training will commence at once. Prince David has a thirty-year head start on you in terms of learning how to run a country."

"And then I wait around for the king to die, and—"

"Assume the throne, yes."

She pushed her plate away. She didn't want to throw up again. "But wait a sec. I read somewhere that the king wants his kids to be co-kings and co-queens. He got the idea from reading *The Lion, the Witch, and the Wardrobe*."

"Yes, he did, and, yes, that is his wish. But Miss Krenski . . ." Mr. Dante's sad bulldog eyes blinked slowly at her. "There must be a High King. Or a High Queen."

"In this case, me."

"In this case, yes. But of course your brothers and sisters would assist you in any way they could."

"*Half* brothers and sisters," she couldn't resist adding.

Mr. Dante tactfully ignored that. "Quite frankly, you cannot be everywhere at once, which His Majesty discovered in his early twenties, and you would be unwise to try. If I may impart a confidence to you, Miss Krenski—"

"Nicole."

"Thank you, Miss Krenski, but no thank you. This is the best I can do until your status as an HRH is confirmed, at which point I—"

"HRH?"

"Her Royal Highness. Are you all right?"

"It's nothing," she said, trying to stifle her gag reflex.

"As I was saying, the king has always regretted being an only child and has taken nothing but joy at the birth of each successive son or daughter. You wrote in your letter that you thought he might be embarrassed by you. Nothing could be further from the truth. He is most anxious to begin the process of knowing you."

Nicole grunted. "Well, he's gonna get his wish, starting tomorrow. But this whole shitstorm? It's gonna be on *my* terms."

Mr. Dante, who seemed like a helluva nice guy in spite of his overly formal demeanor—how did you sit at attention?—shook his head. "Oh, my dear. At this moment, several of your blood relatives are thinking the exact same thing."

She absently cracked her knuckles. "Well, we'll see."

"Miss Krenski, if I may make bold to ask—"

"You ate all the rest of my rice, so you might as well stay bold."

"What on earth has changed your mind? I had a private wager with myself that you would have (a) held out for six more months at least or (b) fled to America."

Her headache, which had finally been receding, gave a tremendous throb, and she nearly barked, "Fled?"

Weirdly, Edmund seemed pleased. "I beg your pardon, I meant no offense. I only thought you might have taken advantage of your dual citizenship."

"Yeah, well. That's over now."

"Over?"

She couldn't tell whether he was being super-tactful or playing dumb. But didn't it come down to the same thing?

"It's in the papers. Local at first, but the wires have jumped on it now. It's spreading all over the world like Ebola squared. My boss blabbed the whole thing."

"I see. Sweet and sour sauce?"

"No, I'll puke again."

"Something we must avoid at all costs."

"This morning when I came to work there were a zillion reporters and even more civilians." She still had trouble understanding the fact that all those strangers wanted to take her picture. Among other things.

"That is to be—"

"Wanting my *autograph*, you believe it? I'll never have a private life again. Everything's—" She heard her voice crack and hated herself for it. She cleared her throat and quietly continued, "Everything's over for me, now. So there's no point in fighting it for another week. Or even another day."

For some reason, Mr. Dante was on his feet and patting

her on the shoulder. "Oh, Highness, don't cry. It's just another beginning. Nothing at all to fear."

It was only then that she realized her face was wet.

And it was only hours later that she realized what he had called her, quite unaware, while comforting her.

She would spend the rest of her life internally flinching at the title, but would never forgot that the first time she heard it it wasn't so bad.

Chapter 17

"Out!" the King of Alaska roared, his hands running across his desk and finally seizing something that wouldn't give him a paper cut. He hurled a paperweight in Holly Bragon's general direction, but as usual, she didn't take the hint. Normally he would never treat a lady in such a fashion, but of course, the Dragon was no lady.

"So!" Holly said as if a glass weight hadn't shattered two feet (he had been careful to aim wide) from her left ear. "Tell me about the bastard princess."

"If you give her that name in my God-be-damned memoirs, I will give you a nose job with a chainsaw."

"Already had one, sans chainsaw," she said, clicking forward on her high heels and sitting in the chair to the left of his desk. "Can't you tell? Don't I look glorious?"

He fought the urge to plunge his hands in his hair and yank. He still had every strand, by God, at an age when lots of men were bald as billiard balls. He wouldn't let her drive him to Rogaine.

The awful thing was, the Dragon *did* look glorious. About fifteen years younger than him, she was a fine-looking, brown-eyed redhead with the lush figure of a fifties pinup girl. None of that anorexia chic for the Dragon.

The only concession to her age were her purple-rimmed bifocals. Her tailored suit was the same shade. When she crossed her legs, he observed that she had not given up the odd habit of wearing tennis shoes with designer suits.

"You look like a Goddamned eggplant in that thing."

"Oh, Big Al, every word out of your mouth is pure honeycomb." Hun-ahh-cooom.

"And you sound like pure cornpone. When are you going to ditch that awful accent?"

"Big Al, I'm gonna give your funeral service in my cornpone accent, and every fellow Texan is gonna cheer me on." Give yer fun'rul sur-vuss. Gone cheer me awn.

He slumped back in his chair and massaged his temples. "God, I think my ears are actually bleeding."

"It's that high-cholesterol lifestyle you lead, big guy. So tell me about the new girl. Word on the wires is, she's a bit older than Davey."

"Prince David."

"O'course, Big Al."

"That's King Al!" Fucking Americans. Too casual by far. Right now, he could stand a little awe.

"Whatever you say, Big Al." She crossed her legs and even the whisper of her pantyhose rubbing together got on his nerves. "Anyhoo, that puts her in line for your job after you fall overboard and drown on one a'your clandestine fishin' trips that don't fool no one no how. Right?"

"Are you speaking English? At all?"

"Ah can speak anuhthin." She occasionally tortured him by deepening her already annoying Texan accent, and could keep it up for hours.

She had been fired nine times.

She had been escorted out by Jeffrey seventeen times.

She had reduced him to shouting at her so many times he

lost count after her second visit. But like roaches and disco, she kept coming back.

And far, far worst of all? The Dragon was his official biographer. She had a doctorate in Alaskan history, gotten published at age nineteen, and written four books on the history of Alaska.

And as usual, the royal family had chosen a foreigner for the job of chronicling the current monarch's life. Subjects tended to be a little too overawed to ask the tough questions.

"So? It's true, raht?"

He rubbed his eyes. "Yes, it's true. I had a—a relationship before I married the queen. Forget it, not tellin'."

"Aw, Big Al, an' here I was on the edge of my seat waiting to hear about your naked shenanigans."

"Shenanigans? Did you just curse me in Texan? Never mind. Point is, yeah, I wasn't exactly a virgin on my wedding night." *Then again, neither was my bride.* "And Nicole Krenski Baranov was the result."

The Dragon didn't write any of that down in her ever-present notebook. "Why, Big Al, I've never known you to go out on a limb. I hear the DNA ain't been confirmed."

"Hasn't been confirmed, you illiterate twit!"

"Thay-ets Daktuh Illiterate Twee-it, Big Al," she corrected him sweetly.

"Okay, okay, stop it, you're killing me. You hear me? After I fired you the fourth time my doctor said my blood pressure was ten points higher than normal! You are *literally* killing me!"

"All part of the big plan, Big Al," she said, easing up on the accent. "I'm the Texan Secret Weapon, sent up here to kill you."

"I fucking knew it!"

"Anyway, like I said, DNA hasn't been confirmed. So why take the risk of telling me?"

"Because I'm old and tired and it's been a weird damned week."

She laughed at him. He made a mental note to check with Parliament to see if he could bomb Texas. "You! Old!" She laughed so hard she almost fell out of her chair. Unfortunately, no such luck. "You! Oh my Gawd! Haw haw haw!"

He surreptitiously checked to make sure his ears hadn't begun to bleed. "You really were sent by America to kill me, weren't you?" he asked gloomily.

"Big Al, the grand ole You Ess of America don't need me. They could turn Juneau into a smokin' pile of cinders with no trouble a'tall. Now. Tell me about the new girl."

"No."

"Aw, Al. You know I'm gonna get it out of you even-'chally."

"Shut up. You will not. Where the hell were we when I last fired your ass?"

She leaned over in her chair and slapped a thigh. "My extremely *shapely* ass, don't pretend you never noticed, and we were talking about how you flew fighters in Korea."

"Right. Okay. So . . ."

Chapter 18

Jeffrey had driven her to Mr. Dante's house, waited silently and patiently in the car—Mr. Dante had never even seen him—then had driven her back home. He had taken in her swollen eyes at a glance and, thank God, said nothing.

She didn't speak a word for forty miles, but weirdly, it wasn't awkward. Jeffrey hummed along with the fifties oldies station he played softly and seemed content to let her think. Or (what she was really doing) stew.

"Come in for a moment?" she asked when he pulled up to her trailer.

"That depends. How's your artillery?"

"Oh, that's hilarious."

"I prefer the word *cautious*."

When they were inside, she offered him a drink, which he declined. Oh . . . duh. He probably considered himself on duty.

"Uh, can you give me a ride to the palace tomorrow?"

He had been glancing around her living room, and spun around so fast she nearly took a step backward. For a big guy, he was quick on his feet. "The palace? You want to go to the palace? *Our* palace?"

"No, Buckingham Palace," she snapped. "Of course our

palace. Can you give me a ride? And get me in to talk to the king?"

"Of course. But as the head of his detail, I'd like to know your intentions. You realize that killing him will only—"

"I'm not going to kill him! My intentions are to submit to a DNA test."

"You're taking a DNA test?"

"Are you partially deaf with that earpiece clogging up your left ear? *Yes*."

She observed his eyebrows knit together. "Tomorrow?"

"Yup." Gorgeous, but slow on the uptake, this guy.

"And then it will be official. You will be, to the world, Her Royal Highness, Crown Princess Nicole."

"I guess."

"Oh. Then I better do this now."

"Do what?"

But he was moving with that lithe speed again and before she knew it, he was holding her in his arms and kissing her on the mouth. She was so surprised she forgot to bite.

And then she pretty much forgot everything else, too, for the first time since this crazy shit started up.

He was holding her firmly, but she had no sense of being restrained. He was taking her mouth without permission, but she had no sense of being violated.

Best of all, he wasn't stopping, and she had no sense of being not in control of the situation.

Because the truth was, she was kissing him back just as hard as he was kissing her.

Finally, after a time that might have been ten seconds or ten minutes, he let go of her and spun away, leaning on the counter between the kitchen and the living room. Clutching the counter, really. She saw with some astonishment that his knuckles were white.

"Why—why did you do that?"

"Because tomorrow you'll be Princess Nicole, and I won't be able to do it. I'll never be able to do it again."

"But—"

"Good night, Nicole."

She was so amazed she forgot to stop him.

Chapter 19

A discreet rap on the door. King Al, grumpy after a long session spilling his life to the Dragon, and five more Buds, and four hours of sleep, massaged his temples. The discreet rap sounded like a giant was pounding on the wood with a ball-peen hammer.

His breakfast sat before him, untouched. At the moment, he doubted he'd ever be able to eat again. And he was swearing off beer! Again!

Another discreet rap.

He made a bet with himself. It would be Edmund, with the morning mail.

"Come in, Edmund."

Only Edmund's head came in; he had opened the door and stuck his head through. "Your Majesty? Drink your juice."

"I fucking hate tomato juice! It's like drinking red snot."

"A master of poetry, even during the largest of hangovers. Majesty, I have a surprise for you."

"Edmund, if I have one more surprise this week, I'm firing you."

"Do not tease, Majesty. Are you ready?"

"Oh God," he sighed. Then, "Hit me."

Edmund's head disappeared, and then Nicole walked in.

"Holy mother of God!"

"It's nice to see you too, Al." Nicole had a wry expression on her face. Cute as a bug, too, and—was she wearing a *dress*? A perfectly lovely dress with black tights and sensible black flats?

"Wh—what—how—why—"

"A man of letters, just like Mr. Dante said. Awesome."

"I have a brain tumor, so please stop yanking my chain," he begged.

"It's just a headache, you infant. Look, I went over to Mr. Dante's house yesterday and talked it over with him and here I am, so shut up about it now."

"But how the hell did you even know where he lived?"

"Who cares? I'm here, right?"

"*Damn* right! Hell, it's great to see you again, kiddo!" He got up and practically ran around his desk, holding his arms out without thinking.

He would have bet the east wing that she had no idea how horrified she looked at that moment, so he dropped his arms and stuck out a hand instead. Thawing an inch or two, she shook it.

"Edmund, you are a fuckin' miracle worker!"

"Yes, Your Majesty." The crumb didn't even bother looking smug. Just took it as his due. "All in a day's work, Your Majesty."

She jerked a thumb in Edmund's direction. "I bet that gets annoying."

"Hon, you have no idea. Nice dress," he said, motioning for her to sit down.

"Thanks. It's the only one I have. Wore it to Mom's memorial service."

"Oh." That would explain the severe black and the long

sleeves. And what message was she sending, anyway? Reminding him he couldn't take her mother's place? That was fine. He'd never intended to try. "Well. Ah. Say, how did you get in here, anyway? You're not anywhere on my schedule." He was pretty sure.

"Jeffrey brought me here."

Fine, but why did that make her blush? Well, it was a stressful moment for her. And not likely to get much better in the months to come. He tried to harden his heart against the sympathy he felt for her (for the good of the country!) and failed. He had never been able to harden his heart against a child. Any child.

"Jeffrey switched with Reynolds this morning," Edmund added. "Which *is* on your schedule."

"I knew that," he bluffed. "So, uh, kiddo—Nicole—if you don't mind, I'd just as soon we got that test out of the way before you change your mind and shoot us all in the face."

Nicole remained a stone. "That's probably a good idea."

"Edmund, will you get doctor—"

"ETA four minutes, my king."

"Oh." Annoying bastard. And thank God. "Great. Nicole, you had anything to eat yet?" He suddenly remembered the paramedics, the ambulance, and felt bad about all the hangover bitching. "How's *your* head?"

"Yes, and fine."

"Oh."

She just sat there like a lump, a pretty lump, and looked at him. Her hands, already tan from being outdoors, rested limply on the chair's armrests. Her long, slender fingers didn't move.

"I'm sure glad you're here," he said again, totally at a loss. He could deal with kids. He could deal with *his* kids. He could deal with his grown-up kids. But a grown up kid he'd known only for a week? That was breaking new territory.

Al mentally spat on his hands. The blood of rebels ran in his veins, and they had made an art form of breaking new territory.

It did not occur to him until much later that the blood of rebels ran in *her* veins, too.

"You don't want anything? Cup of coffee? Tea? Milkshake? Soy shake? Latte? A beer and a ball?"

"It's a little early for me, so never mind the booze, but I'd kill for a cup of coffee," she admitted. "Where is it? I'll get it myself."

"No, no, Edmund will get it."

One of her fingers twitched. Her trigger finger, he noticed. Her eyes narrowed a bit and her mouth thinned. "I'm not gonna be waited on hand and foot, King Alexander. So you can get that idea out of your pounding head right now."

"Of course not, we'd never dream of radically altering your lifestyle," Edmund broke in. "How do you take it, Miss Krenski?"

She sighed and he figured she'd already guessed there was no arguing with the man. "Black."

"Atta girl," he couldn't help but say. "She takes it like a man," he couldn't help bragging to Edmund.

"Your exquisite notions of chauvinism are as fascinating as they are maddening, my king."

Nicole laughed for the first time that day.

"Shaddup," he told them both.

Chapter 20

"Match," the doc whose name Al couldn't remember told him. "Match. And match."

"Don't talk in your medical jargon, doc; just spell it out."

"Oh." The doctor frowned. "I thought I was being fairly clear. Miss Krenski is a direct blood relation of yours, Your Majesty, a sibling or a daughter. And due to the age difference and the fact that your parents are—"

"Right. So it's official. She's my daughter."

"She is, Your Majesty. There is no doubt."

"There never was, doc."

He was so excited to get the ball moving, he didn't notice his youngest, Nicholas, motioning to the doctor. He went out the door of the lab without another backward glance, to his son's great good fortune.

Part Two

BASTARD PRINCESS

Chapter 21

SITKA PALACE CONFIRMS BASTARD PRINCESS
NEXT IN LINE FOR THRONE

Nicole walked into yet another ridiculously grand room, one she could have fit four of her trailers in. Her (ugh) siblings and (ugh ugh) father were already seated.

"Hey, Nicole," Nicholas, the youngest, called to her. He was the only blonde among them. She'd heard the rumors, of course.

The official story was that Queen Dara was killed in a car accident on the way to a hairdresser appointment. Unofficially, she had been en route to meet her lover—Nicky's real father.

But even when things were at their worst—when David and Christina were king and queen *pro tem* while King Alexander was in a coma—David did not permit a DNA test for the youngest Baranov.

"You made the front page this morning," Nicholas was saying. "Again."

"No reading at the table," King Al ordered. "Ditch the rag, boy. How'd you sleep, Nicole?"

"Fine." A lie. "But if I'm going to live here, is there a chance I could pick a different bedroom?"

"You can have any room—rooms—you want."

Excellent.

"You hungry? You must be. I didn't see you eat a thing all day yesterday."

"Sure." There was one empty spot at the table—to the king's right. David sat at his left. "Thanks for waiting for me. Let's eat."

"Hallelujah, brothers. And sisters," Alexander, the middle son, said. "Nicole, can I ask a personal question?"

"Sure."

"What happened to your mama?"

Before Nicole could reply, Kathryn, the youngest daughter, hurled a croissant across the table, catching Alexander neatly on the upper lip. "Dumbass! Don't ask her *that*."

"Cancer," Nicole replied, struggling to remain straight-faced.

"Was she in any pain at the end?" the king asked quietly, which neatly quashed her urge to laugh.

"No, at the end—she never knew anything."

"Asshole!" Alexandria, the eldest daughter (besides Nicole herself, she supposed), hissed at her brother. "Our first meal as a family and you had to go bring *that* up! Throw something else, Kathryn."

"I'm sorry, I'm sorry!" Alexander was cowering behind his saucer. "I was curious, that's all. I would have liked to have met her. That's all."

"She got the diagnosis about two years ago," Nicole elaborated, helping herself to an English muffin. "I took care of her as long as I could."

"*You* took care of her?" Christina asked.

"No, I slammed her ass in a nursing home so I wouldn't

be bothered," Nicole snapped, feeling her cheeks get warm.

"Please don't kill my wife," David said calmly, spooning up oatmeal. "It'll ruin Christmas."

Nicole laughed; she couldn't help it.

"You're, uh, kinda mercurial, aren't you?" Kathryn asked.

Nicole shrugged, and as a footman discreetly poured her coffee, she thanked him and took a sip.

Her first night in the palace had been strange. She'd known it would be, of course, but still wasn't prepared.

For one thing, the palace was ginormous. Easily the largest building she'd been in in her life—and she used to live in L.A. With hallways and rooms and corridors and multiple kitchens and nine thousand fireplaces, and it went on and on and on.

For another, she had a real glimpse of the kindness of the king. Her father. There had been a press conference, but she hadn't attended. Mr. Dante and her dad had handled the whole thing.

He had told her to explore and gave her a cell phone so small and thin it looked more like a fat credit card than anything else.

It had a very specific function; it summoned intermediaries at a beep, particularly Edmund.

So she had walked around and occasionally bumped into a sibling and introduced herself to at least a hundred staff members, and by the time she went looking for David, he was long gone and not due back until after midnight. She and Christina had exchanged a few stiff words, she'd declined to meet her niece, and left.

Exhausted, she had gone to bed in a palatial (no pun intended) room that screamed "anonymous guest bedroom."

Well, at least they didn't already have a suite in her name all set up. They were arrogant, but not that arrogant.

And now they were, day two, at breakfast.

She had hoped to talk to David alone, then realized it might be a thing better spoken in front of all of them, so she spoke her piece.

"I'm sorry about usurping the throne from you," she said, taking another sip of the excellent coffee. "That's not why I wrote the letter."

"Usurp means to seize or commandeer," Alexander-the-younger said, "implying you had no right to it. When, in fact, you have every right to it."

David was nodding. They—they were *all* nodding. *That* was a shock. "Still. I'm sorry."

"I'm sorry, too, Nicole, but not for the reasons you think. None of this can be easy for you. We'll all do our best to make the transition as painless as possible."

"Ha," she murmured, looking down at her plate.

"As for not being king . . . I haven't really had a chance to wrap my brain around that one." He smiled, but the smile didn't climb into his eyes. "But who can predict the future? Who knows? Maybe Dad has another kid running around and he or she is older than you are. Then you're off the hook."

She smiled. "Tease."

"I'm sitting right here, kids."

"Sorry, Dad," David replied. "But you're not exactly lily white on this one."

"I gotta take shit from a punk like you?"

"I know!" Nicky said, squeezing his muffin so hard it imploded in a spray of crumbs and blueberries. "The day Dad dies, Nicole can abdicate! Then everything will go back to the way it was."

"I'm *sitting* right *here*."

"My mother didn't raise me to shirk my responsibilities," Nicole said quietly, and that was the end of that.

Chapter 22

"Hi!" a cheerful redhead about ten years older than Nicole said. "I'm Holly Bragon, rhymes with dragon. I'm the king's official biographer."

"Hi." Nicole shook hands with the woman.

"I don't suppose you're in the mood to talk about your mother."

"Not hardly."

"Or how all this feels right now?"

"Nuh-uh."

"Or what it's like to go from a commoner to first in line for the throne, set to inherit one of the world's largest fortunes?"

"Nope."

"I figured." The redhead looked around the suite of rooms. "Is this gonna be yours, then?"

"Guess so."

"A taciturn girl, I like that. The others can be a bit of a handful."

"Not me. I'm a pussycat."

"Yeah, and I'm an amoeba."

Holly pushed past Nicole—a relief from bowing and "Your Highness" this and "Your Highness" that. Nicole pegged her accent as deep South United States, Texas or Georgia or someplace like that.

Holly peered out the five-foot-high windows. "Hmmm. It looks like we're three stories up, but the south pavilion roof is right down there, ain't it? And from there it's not much of a drop for a tall girl like you."

Nicole raised her eyebrows. Holly "rhymes with dragon" was a quick one. "Really? I hadn't noticed."

"My big ole Texan butt you hadn't." She slapped herself on the flank. "Ain't it great?"

"Uh . . . it's very nice."

"But if I had to make that drop, I'd mess up my fabulous underwear. Heights give me the creeps. But not you, I bet."

"I once followed a bear over a cliff."

"I'm making a memo to me to follow up with you on that story. But why?"

"Well, I shot him but didn't kill him, so I was morally obligated to—"

"No, no. Why this suite, why the setup so you can slip off the grounds? You're not a prisoner, like Rapunzel in her tower."

"I like to come and go as I like. Do you have any idea how long it takes just to arrange to go into town for, I dunno, a cup of coffee?"

"I got an idea."

"First you gotta tell Edmund. Then he tells your security detail. Then they waste tons of time getting organized. Then, an hour or two later, finally, you can leave. Except you're not alone, of course. And with all the bodyguards and royal cars and all, everybody stares. And you can't pay for anything; the store owner comes out and practically genuflects. Then, finally, you come back to the gilded cage."

"Prob'ly easier to stay in and have someone bring you a cuppa joe."

"That's not the point. The point is, I used to be able to come and go as I please, and now I can't." She resisted the urge to kick something. "Rapunzel's got nothing on me."

"Poor baby," the Dragon yawned. "How do you find the strength to go on?"

"Now you're just messing with me."

The Dragon turned and beamed at her. "It's what I do, darlin'. Excuse me: Princess Darlin'. So if you don't mind my asking, what's next for you?"

"Princess lessons, I guess. Maybe smashing champagne bottles on a few cruise ships."

"Well, there's worse royal families to end up in, you ask me."

"That's hard to imagine."

"Ha! Honey, I'm a history major and a writer. Know what that makes me? The biggest snoop you ever met."

"With a wonderful ass."

"Well, yeah. And historically speaking, most princesses were ugly and dumb from all the inbreeding."

"What a lovely thought," she said, appalled.

"History ain't lovely, honey. At least in this country, they don't much care if you marry one a' the *hoi polloi*."

"I have noticed they're all ridiculously good looking," she admitted. "Guess it pays not to keep marrying your cousin."

"Check your mirror sometime, honey, speaking of ridiculous."

"Well, biggest snoop I ever met, expert on the royal family, I have to admit I'm curious about something."

"Shoot, darlin'."

"What's your theory about Prince Nicky's parentage?"

Holly snapped her notebook shut and gave Nicole a look over her bifocals. "That's generally considered the rudest question you can ask in these here parts. You want to get along with your new family, I wouldn't bring it up. Ever."

"Thanks for the advice."

The sunny smile returned. "All part of the service, darlin'."

Chapter 23

Jeffrey had spent the last two hours guarding Nicole's closed bedroom door, then went to stroll the grounds on a break. And like a lovesick school boy, he was standing on the lawn beneath Nicole's suite, staring up at the windows.

Get it together, man.

He'd had flings before. He'd even been in love before. But no one had ever made him feel like this. Hot and cold and urgent and lusty and protective and angry and happy all at once or one right after the other.

It was . . . disconcerting.

He doubted Nicole had a clue. He prayed she didn't have a clue. It was too embarrassing, almost a cliché; he was not in a Whitney Houston movie, for the love of God. And he outweighed Kevin Costner by forty pounds.

While he watched the window, he thought about the kiss. Thought about her scent—she smelled like the outdoors, fresh and cottony—and her sweetly yielding mouth. Thought about how he almost took her on the floor of her living room like a—like a—

He tried to shake it off. Never had he been so easily distracted while on duty; it was shameful. He was doing her no good if all he could think about was how she looked without her—

Now what the hell was *this*?

The darkened window was silently swinging open and he grabbed for his gun out of pure ingrained training. Which would have been fine if someone was going *in*.

Instead, a lithe figure in dark clothes climbed out, hung from her hands by the sill, and dropped almost noiselessly to the roof of the pavilion. Swung over again, hung until her legs only dangled about four-and-a-half feet above the ground, and dropped yet again. Then stood, looked around, and walked away without the slightest trace of a limp.

He holstered his gun and nearly fell to his knees, his relief was so great. The twit could have broken every bone in her body! Talk about your personal and professional disasters. He could imagine the conversation: "My king, the first night I was in charge of Princess Nicole's detail, she broke both her legs. Very sorry."

He stepped out of the shadows to intercept her. "Going somewhere, Your Highness?"

"Gaaaaah! Jeez! Don't *do* that!"

"So very sorry, Your Highness."

"Jeffrey, you bum, were you watching my window?"

"Of course. You didn't think we just hung around in doorways, did you?"

Hands on her hips, she advanced on him. He wondered how heavily armed she was. "I just want to take a walk, get it? And I don't want to bring the whole damn circus along, either."

"How about just me, Your Highness?"

She chewed on her lip, which made him want to chew on her lip, and finally said, "Well, I s'pose. Let's hit the bricks."

"Thank you, Highness."

"Like you wouldn't rat me out if I didn't let you tag along."

"So astute, Your Highness."

"And that's another thing. I *saw* you yesterday. On your break." They were walking across the vast lawn, staying out of the pools of brightness cast by the floodlights. "Doing the *New York Times* crossword."

She saw him? Well, that seemed fair, as he was acutely aware whenever she was within twenty yards of him. "Yes?"

"In ink."

"I was all out of chisels."

"But I've seen footmen treat you like your knuckles drag on the ground when you walk."

"I know. Isn't it splendid?"

She stared at him, then laughed. "Ah. Ah-ha! I get it. Me big dumb bodyguard, me easily tricked, come into my web said the spider to the fly."

"Or words to that effect," he agreed, hands in his pockets so he wouldn't grab her for another kiss. "Let them think what they like. Let them assume a man my size is slow and/or stupid. I like it when they can't see me coming."

"Now that's a philosophy I can get behind," she said approvingly, and he grinned in the dark. "So where'd you learn to fish?"

"My dad, when he wasn't guarding the late king and queen. His dad before him. How about you?"

"I found guides and they taught me. I've spent more of my life in Los Angeles than Alaska, but I was always . . . I don't know . . . pulled?"

"Pulled," he agreed. It was as fine a word for duty as any. Duty to country, or to self.

"I always wanted trees and rivers and green. I feel like there's a plan when I'm in the forest instead of all this—this"—she gestured vaguely and he wondered if she realized she was pointing at the palace—"chaos."

"They're a noisy bunch," he said quietly, "and they've got tempers like you wouldn't believe. Or perhaps you would. But they're good people. There's a reason nobility comes from the word *noble*. The Baranovs showed me that when I was still a child."

"Wow, Jeffrey, sounds like you've got a serious case of man-love," she teased.

He didn't crack a smile. "They take nothing for granted; not their wealth, not our service. Nothing. And if someone shot me, he'd have his hands full with my king. I can dedicate my lives to them because they have dedicated theirs to mine."

She chewed on that one for a moment, then added, "Really noisy. Hair-trigger tempers."

"Pot, meet kettle. Kettle, meet pot."

"Oh, hush up. You and your unanswerable observations." She was cupping her elbows and he realized that she was wearing only black leggings, flats, and a black T-shirt, and the sun had set two hours ago. He unbuttoned his suit jacket and slung it over her shoulders.

"Thanks. Stupid not to bring a jacket. Except I didn't have a black one." She pushed her arms into the sleeves and huddled into it. "Hey, maybe I would have frozen to death and then wouldn't have to worry about any of this."

"How nice that my career would have ended on a note of personal disaster, not to mention total disgrace."

"Hey, nobody asked you to skulk outside my window."

"I've been transferred to your detail," he said, not telling her he'd slammed the paperwork through himself. Not telling her that the thought of someone else guarding her made him physically ill. "You don't have to ask me to skulk. Skulking is what I do."

"Great." She kicked at a tuft of grass. "What, you get demoted? That's a bummer."

"Not . . . quite demoted, Highness."

"Nih. Cole. Nicole. *Nicole!* You're wasting your time, you know. I thought you realized when we met that I could take care of myself."

"Nicole Krenski, private citizen? No question. Her Royal Highness the Princess Nicole? The world is a big place, and there are an awful lot of people who wouldn't mind seeing you hurt. Or ransomed." *Or dead.*

"I'm the same person I was two weeks ago," she argued.

"Yes, Princess Nicole. To that end, you're the same person you were thirty years ago: Princess Nicole."

"My mom was right not to tell me," she muttered. "She was right to protect me from all this."

"Your mother kept you from your rightful inheritance, from your destiny. And for what? To keep you to herself."

Nicole swung around and even in the near-gloom he could see her blue eyes blaze. "Do not *ever* shit on my mother, Jeffrey, unless you'd like a pistol-provided enema."

"If I have angered Her Highness, I apologize."

"And stop talking about me in the third person!"

"A thousand apologies." He paused and swallowed a snicker. "To Her Highness."

This time the kick landed on his left shin, after which she spent a full minute hobbling in a small circle and groaning, "Ow my God, oh ouch oh ow ow ouch ouch ouch *ouch*!"

"Do you require a doctor, ma'am?"

"No fucking doctor! Jeffrey, you are driving me *batshit.*"

"A thousand apologies."

"Well, that's two thousand for me, then. And we're never going to talk about it again, are we?"

"Talk about what?" he said, playing dumb, which he did almost as well as Edmund.

"This," she said, and caught him by the hair and pulled him down to her for a kiss that he thought might burn his mouth.

Chapter 24

They grappled, groped, and danced back and forth on the lawn, their mouths together, their tongues dueling, until Nicole lost her balance, Jeffrey lost his trying to grab for her, and they both rolled all the way down the south lawn.

How steep is *this hill*? she had time to wonder before fetching up against the trunk of a tree, hard.

She groaned.

"Nicole?" His face peered anxiously down at her, feeling her limbs, the back of her skull. "Are you all right? Do you need a doc—"

"No . . . fucking . . . doctors," she moaned, wondering if he'd even realized he'd dropped the "Her Highness" crap. "Had my fill while I was watching my mom die." She sat up and observed the line of pine trees marking the edge of the lawn. "Oh, man, I hope you've got a crane in one of your pockets. I don't think I can get back up that hill on my own."

"Why—why did you do that?"

"Because I'm clumsy and I don't know the lay of the land."

"Not that. Why did you kiss me?"

She extended a hand, more to feel his than anything else, and he pulled her easily to her feet. "Why did you kiss *me*?"

"I told you why. Once you're officially a princess—"

"Screw that, Jeffrey. Do you know how long it's been since I got laid?"

He gaped at her.

"Well?"

Still he stared.

"Going on two years, buddy boy. And if you think I'm gonna be The Celibate Princess, your tailor's been cutting your suits too tight."

"I—I—I—"

"Put it this way. You can do me, or you can find someone to do me. Y'know, vet their credentials, make sure they're not a security risk. That sort of thing. Either that or I keep sneaking out of the castle at odd times of the day and night looking for lurrrrrv."

Even in the gloom, she could see him whiten. "You—you—you—"

"Are you sure you're the smart one?"

"My IQ is 157," he snapped, brushing pine needles out of his hair, "and you're telling me I've got to fuck you or pimp you?"

"Wow, that's quite a turn of phrase, Big Brain. But, yeah. That's what I'm telling you."

He threw up his hands and walked around in a small circle. "You're just as bad as any of them!"

"Oh, hey. No need to get nasty."

"My way or the highway." Now he was kicking grass. "It ought to be on the Baranov coat of arms."

"What *is* on the Baranov coat—"

"Nicole, I can't."

"Oh. Old war injury?" She swallowed a giggle as she saw him flush.

"I didn't mean I physically can't—couldn't—I mean I'm perfectly capable—that is, the ladies have said—not that there have been a lot, but—oh, fuck."

That was it; it was too much. Overload. She sank to her knees, laughing like a loon on uppers.

"I remind Her Highness," he said grimly, hands jammed wrist-deep into his pockets, "that I am heavily armed."

"Prove it, stud. And stop talking about me in the third person; I'm not warning you again. But first get me up this hill."

"I'll do the latter, but we're not done discussing the first."

"How about if I make it a royal command?"

"You couldn't issue a royal command if I stuck my gun up your nose."

"Oooh, is that your idea of foreplay?"

Muttering, he turned his back to her and brushed more pine needles off his suit. She leaped on his back and wrapped her legs around his waist. He was so surprised he nearly fell down again.

"Let's ride, cowboy," she said, then kissed him on the right earlobe.

He took the gradual slope at a dead run, clutching her legs so she wouldn't fall off, and she rode him all the way to the top, whooping and giggling.

They were having so much fun, in fact, that they nearly knocked Edmund down the same slope they'd just come up.

Chapter 25

Jeffrey had his gun out, but whether it was to shoot himself, Nicole, or Edmund he didn't know.

Disgrace. Dishonor. Death?

Edmund's question, "Did you two lose something besides your minds?" was still hanging in the air.

Nicole hadn't climbed down. She just glared at Edmund over Jeffrey's left shoulder. He could *feel* the glare.

"What are you doing out here? It's practically the middle of the night!"

"It's nine thirty," Edmund said mildly. "Prince Nicholas went looking for you, Princess. He is still looking. So I suggest, Your Highness, that you get back inside. Now."

It was amazing. He sounded totally polite, even deferential, but she knew it wasn't a request.

Jeffrey, the bum who was *supposedly* watching out for her physical safety, dropped her like she was hot, and she hit the lawn ass-first.

"Ow, dammit!" Nicole reacted. Then, "Fine, we're going."

"Mr. Dante—"

"Jeffrey, your . . . ah . . . devotion to duty is commendable, but I am perfectly capable of escorting Her Highness back to the palace if you need to . . . ah . . . walk the perimeter. That *is* what you were doing, yes?" He speared Jeffrey with a laser-beam gaze. "Walking the perimeter?"

"Yes."

"Very well. Good night."

"Good night," Jeffrey said glumly. There was no point in wondering whether Edmund had seen them kissing. The man saw *everything*.

"Hey." Nicole was handing him back his jacket. "You're not in trouble, right? Because I take full responsibility. I was the one who climbed out of my window and—"

"I enjoyed our walk, Highness," he said loudly, drowning out her confession. "Reynolds will relieve me at the top of the hour, and I'll see you tomorrow."

"Oh."

Incredibly, she seemed almost hurt. But that couldn't be right. He was saving her reputation at the cost of his own. It was for her own good. Surely she realized that.

"Fine. See ya," Nicole said.

She fell into step with Edmund and walked with him without once looking back.

He knew, because he was watching.

Chapter 26

Prince Nicholas, last in line for the throne, was giving serious thought to playing baseball with the jade chess pieces the Emperor had given his great-grandfather when Edmund finally walked in with Nicole.

Edmund, of course, looked as he always did: starched and proper. Edmund was never-ending, like the tides, and never-changing, like the face of the moon, or his father, or Kathryn's aim.

But Nicole looked like she'd been run over by a truck. Her hair was all over the place, there was something sticky (sap? mud?) on her left cheek, pine needles all over her leggings, a bloody scratch on her right arm, and her mouth looked weird, like the lips were slightly swollen or something.

"Holy crap! What happened to you?"

"A midnight hike," she said. "Thanks for the escort, Edmund. Buh-bye."

"Highnesses." Edmund bowed and left.

Nicole looked around the room, noting the several dozen chess boards. "Oh, boy. The boredom generated in this room alone is trying to sap my will to live." She turned her gaze—so like his other sisters—on him. "You were looking for me?"

This was a pleasant surprise. His other siblings took their sweet time when he needed one of them or were busy on one royal duty or another. He was the baby; he was used to the teasing and, worse, being ignored.

And Nicole was really old, older even than David! Mid thirties! That was *old*, man. He couldn't believe he had to wait only ten minutes for her to show up.

"I knocked on your door but you didn't answer, so I thought you were sleeping. But Edmund said he knew where you were. It's kind of cold out for hiking, isn't it?" he asked, puzzled.

"That depends," she replied, "on who you're hiking with. What's up, blondie?"

"Nothing."

"That's why I got hauled into the Room of Perpetual Yawns? For nothing?"

"I just—I was just hoping you were doing okay."

She gave him an odd look and sat down across from him. They both ignored the chess board between them. "As well as can be expected, I guess."

"If I had to go live in a strange place, I might be scared. And I prob'ly wouldn't tell anybody if I *was* scared. And it's okay. If you're scared, I mean."

"I'm fine."

"Also," he added, holding out a CD case, "there's this."

She took it and examined it. "What is it? Did you burn me a mix CD? Because I have to tell you, I'm all eighties rock, all the time."

"Wow, you really *are* old."

"What a wonderful conversation we're having," she muttered, and he felt bad because he forgot old people didn't like being reminded they were old. "If this isn't The Greatest Hits of Teena Marie, then what is it?"

"The nineteen ways I've found to get safely out of the palace without being seen. You keep going over the ledge like that and off the pavilion, you're going to break an ankle."

She stared at him. "Does everyone know that's why I picked that suite?"

"Just me and Edmund. And probably your security detail. And maybe the Dragon. Probably the Dragon."

"If he didn't, he sure does now," she muttered, which he didn't quite get. "Does the king know?"

"No, *our father* doesn't know. Are you kidding? He still thinks Kathryn's a virgin."

Her eyes nearly bulged out of her head. "Thaaaat's a bit of an overshare. Let's not do that again, okay? Okay."

"Now I'm the only virgin in the family," he added glumly.

"You just did it again!"

"Well, I am."

"Don't sweat it. Sex is overrated."

"Really?" His brothers and sisters *never* talked to him about this stuff. Why would they? To him, he was always going to be the six-year-old mischief maker who didn't look like any of them. "You don't like it?"

"I didn't say that, I just said it's overrated. Look, when you're a virgin, losing it is the most important thing in the world. It's all you can think about, right? But once it's gone, once you've got that whole awkward weird first time out of the way, it's never going to be as big a deal again."

Except she had an odd look on her face as she told him this, almost like she wasn't sure she believed what she was saying.

"Hard to imagine," he sighed.

"Trust me, this aged ancient knows of what she speaks. Dammit! Now *I'm* referring to myself in the third person." She bounced the case up and down in her hand like a baseball. "Thanks for this. I owe you one."

"Damn right! So keep it in mind."

"Don't sweat it, Curly. I never forget a favor."

"Of course you don't. You're one of us. And don't call me Curly."

"Or what?"

"Or I'll blow up half of your personal belongings."

"Yeah, listen, what is it with you and incendiary devices? Is it the typical youngest-seeking-attention thing? Or do you, uh, need to be speaking to someone? Someone with many degrees in psychiatry?"

"Not telling."

"You'll tell, Curly."

"Don't call me Curly."

"Oh, never again, Curly." Then she hauled him out of the chair, bounced him to the floor, and tickled him until tears were streaming down his face and he was begging her to stop.

"This might not entirely suck," she announced as he staggered to his feet. "I never had a little brother before."

"I'm three inches taller than you are!"

"Yeah, but your muscle mass hasn't caught up with your height. So until then I can beat you with impunity." She shoved him and he nearly went sprawling, scattering chess pieces like confetti. "And I shall."

"This *does* entirely suck," he informed her, lying like mad. "The last thing I needed was another older sibling."

"Suck it up, Curly."

"Don't call me—don't tickle! No! I mean it! Quit! Nicoooooole!"

Chapter 27

King Al tiptoed through the outer room leading to his office, not an easy thing for a man of his height, or weight.

Moving as stealthily as he could ever remember in his life, he eased the door open and slipped inside. This early, no one was likely to—

"Howdy, Big Al!"

Shit. "You! I fired you yesterday. Again! I made sure Reynolds got you on that flight! You're supposed to be in Dallas right this second."

"Honey, I'm from Houston. And o'course your man saw me get on board. But we refueled in Minot, and I hopped a flight back."

"Shit."

"Once we were back in the U.S. of A., your men didn't have any authority over me. But you knew I couldn't stay away, else why all the pussyfooting at this ungodly hour?"

"I was hedging my bets. Now get lost, you hideous scribe of a she-devil."

"Dragon," she said, smiling. She was wearing the usual purple glasses, this time with a red suit and white jogging shoes. She jiggled her left foot like mad. "And congrats; I didn't know you knew a great big word like scribe."

"How big can it be? It's one syllable."

"Talked to the new girl yesterday," she added, apropos of nothing. "Seems like a nice enough gal."

"You talked to Nicole?" He gestured to a chair. "Siddown, what's your rush? How's she doing? What'd she say?"

"You're askin' me? You're the daddy."

"I'm—I'm trying to give her some space. We've asked a lot of her this week. I don't—I don't want to make things worse."

The Dragon's mouth, normally set in a jeering smile, softened. "She'll come around, Big Al. Who'd resist your charms?"

"Very funny," he grumped. "So what'd she say?"

"Oh, we mostly talked about the historical prevalence of inbreeding among royalty."

Al groaned.

"Well, not in your family, o'course."

He groaned again. "Thanks for that."

"And we talked about her new digs. She sure looks like you guys. And acts like you guys. But—"

"Yeah?"

The Dragon appeared, of all things, to be choosing her words carefully. "She's still missing her mama, o'course."

"Well, naturally."

"And that's why you'll have a hard time. Not because of all this." She gestured to the magnificent office, and the king knew she meant all of it—the money, the status, the property. "But because she lost the only family she ever had. So why would she ever dare let any of y'all get close?"

The king stared at her. "You're pretty smart, for a psychopath."

"Aw." The Dragon winked. "That's what all the cute boys say."

Chapter 28

"Jeffrey, would you mind?"

"Not at all, Highness." Her bodyguard stepped back and kicked in the door to the Outer Banks Co.

"Thanks, Jeffrey."

"My pleasure, Your Highness."

Nicole brushed splinters off her shoulders and marched inside. "Freeborg, you scumbag!"

Her former boss had shoved his chair back as far as he could go without actually going out the window. He was pale, even for him. "Nicole, what—you—I mean, Your Highness—"

"You ratted me out! You blabbed to the press! You ruined my life!"

"But Nicole—I mean, Your Highness—it was going to come out anyway! We had royalty in here two days in a row! I just thought—"

"You thought you'd give this tin-shit operation some much-needed publicity. Never mind that you sold me down the river at the same time."

"But they all—I mean, the royal family all knew you were—"

"Yes, but they couldn't prove it unless their own doctor

did the test. Something I was managing to avoid very neatly, by the way. Until you wrecked any chance I had of a normal life." She was leaning over his desk now, and he was cringing back in his chair. Since he had seen her shoot, this was a wise move. "So I figure the least you deserve is a wrecked door and the penalty of my displeasure."

Jeffrey whispered in her ear. She smiled. Her former boss went, if possible, whiter. "The penalty of *our* displeasure. That's the royal 'our,' by the way."

"Nic—Your Highness, give me a break. Except for the occasional Sandra Dee, we're struggling to stay out of the red. Now I've got bookings through the end of next year!"

"And all you had to do," she said sweetly, "was sell us down the river." Hmm. She could get used to the "royal we" thing. "Well, enjoy your success, Mike. You've earned it. By the way, don't be surprised if you're audited every month until the end of time."

"You wouldn't."

"Hello, have we met? Jeffrey, we're out of here."

"Hey, you were never exactly Employee of the Month!" Freeborg yelled back. "With *that* mouth?"

"Feel better?" Jeffrey murmured, tapping his earpiece.

"Loads," she said, and smiled at him.

Chapter 29

Back in the car, Jeffrey tapped his earpiece again. "Rodinov and Hunter en route to the palace." He listened, then tapped it again.

Nicole figured it was a two-way communication piece, kind of like the ones they used in the old *Star Trek: The Next Generation* episodes. Tap to open broadcast, tap to close. Neat.

"Hunter, huh?"

"That's your call sign."

"Why not just use my name?"

"Because then the bad guys will know who we're talking about."

She mused in the passenger seat. She had flatly refused to ride in the back like an invalid. "What's the king's call sign?"

"Warrior."

"Alexander's?"

"Poet."

Poet? Weird. "Alexandria's?"

"Sleepwalker."

Weirder and weirder. "David's?"

"Mini-Me."

"Oh, that's *good*. Christina's?"

"Cookie."

"Kathryn's?"

"Mime."

What the blue hell? Those were some pretty fucked up call signs. "Nicholas?"

"Rebel."

"Well, all you have to do is read *People* to figure that one out." She was forgetting someone, she just knew—ah! Alexandria had married an American two years ago, but he was currently out of the country. In fact, Alex herself was leaving tomorrow to be with him, according to the schedule.

Yeah, the schedule. She got one of her very own, first thing in the morning, along with all the major newspapers. Every little thing any of the family had to do was spelled out in excruciatingly dull detail. Every morning. With hourly updates.

"So!" she said brightly. "Given any thought to our little chat last night?"

"You mean the chat and the piggyback ride that almost got me fired?"

"Nobody's firing you without my say-so. Wait a minute. If I fire you, will you sleep with me?"

"Do you hear yourself?"

"All too well. Never mind, that'd mean you could sue me for sexual harassment. I'd hate to inadvertently bring a lawsuit against the royal family my first week in residence."

"You've never done anything inadvertently."

"Well, thank you. Neither have they."

"The royal family. Them. They."

"What? Did you skip breakfast? Blood sugar a little low?"

"Your royal family. Us. We."

"Yeah, well, give me time. Anyway, quit trying to change the subject. Have you thought about our chat or haven't you?"

Jeffrey, who usually drove like a robot, actually took his gaze off the road and looked at her. "It's all I've thought about. I didn't sleep a wink last night."

"Really? That's odd. I slept great." And she had, because *she* hadn't slept a wink the night before. "So? What's it going to be?"

"Ni—Your Highness, there's a car behind us with two more bodyguards in it. You want me to just—to just pull over and do you?"

"In a perfect world," she admitted, "yes."

"In a perfect world . . ."

"What?"

"Never mind."

"Come on, spit it out."

"In a perfect world you wouldn't be a princess and I wouldn't be your subject," he said in a rush of words.

"Jeez, take a breath or you're gonna pass out at the wheel."

He did as she asked, he took a deep breath and tightened his grip on the wheel. She was surprised the wheel didn't creak from the pressure.

"And for the record," she added, "I agree one hundred percent. But we're not in a perfect world. If we were, my mom would be alive and French fries would help you lose weight."

He barked a laugh.

"But we're not. And she isn't. And they don't. So what's the plan?"

"The plan is, I drive you back to the Sitka Palace, Princess, and then you do as you will."

"Like that, is it?"

"Yes, it's like that."

"Too bad. I get the feeling we would have been pretty good between the sheets."

"I, too," he said quietly, and wouldn't speak to her for the rest of the drive.

Chapter 30

"You sure you're ready for this, kiddo?"

"Sure, Al."

"Because we can put it off for a few more days. It's no problem."

"It's a huge problem; they're already waiting for us."

The king snorted. He was actually dressed up in a tailored navy blue suit, sky blue shirt, and red-and-blue-striped tie. "Believe me, they'll come back."

"Dad, she wants to do it," David said, equally dressed to the nines. "Let her do it."

"It's fine, Al." "Al" was as close as Nicole could come. She had dropped the "king" but couldn't bring herself to call him Dad, or even Father. "Let's go."

They were in a spacious salon, and sun streamed through the Eastern windows. The king was there, she was there, and David was there. And their bodyguards were there, of course. Also the redhead who, wonderfully, seemed to irritate the piss out of Al.

The other royals had other duties or had gotten out of this one.

Nicole also was dressed in a suit; her closet had mysteriously filled overnight with clothes that fit perfectly. She was dressed in black, with a white blouse and her mother's gold earrings.

The Alaskan Olympic Ski Team marched in, fresh from two silvers and a gold at the Winter Olympics in Gstaad. Nicole, David, and Al were supposed to pat them on the back, have a nice lunch, and in general tell them they were the pride of Alaska.

Which, to be fair, they were.

Nicole sighed and prepared to be bored.

She wasn't bored. Not at all. Because the Olympian on her left—Yanos somebody—and the one across the table from her—Thomas somebody—were both excellent flirts with truly marvelous physiques.

They were full of charming questions about her status as the bastard princess (The papers had given her the nickname, and it had stuck . . . and she didn't mind. It was better than just princess.) and what she had been up to and how she was coping.

"Truly remarkable," Thomas somebody was saying. "And how are you adjusting to life at the palace?"

"Oh, you know. Good days and bad. Hey, don't hog the last roll."

"As my princess commands," Thomas teased, and tossed it to her.

"Very funny, Skier Boi. So what do you guys do when you're not shushing down mountains?"

"Beguile beautiful women," Yannos teased.

"And beg for their favors," Thomas added.

"Beg for their favors? What century do you live in?"

"Any century where you are, Highness."

"Really?" Hmm. She was eating with two men who were literally the best in the world at what they did, who had the bodies of gods and, one hoped, appetites to match. "I don't suppose one of you guys would be open to a royal command, huh?"

"We would be open to anything Your Highness wishes."

"Some things more than others," Thomas asked, giving her a wicked grin.

Now this she could get used to. "Oh! In *that* case, I—shit! I dropped one of my eight forks."

"Here, Princess, you can use mine to—"

"Code twenty-nine!" Jeffrey bellowed. Then he yanked Thomas's chair away from the table, yanked Thomas out of said chair, and tossed him four feet through the air. The skier hit the wooden floor with a spectacular slam.

Nicole saw that the other royals had been hauled away from the table and their guards were standing protectively in front of them.

"What the *hell*?" the king roared, spraying soup.

"He was trying to stab the princess," Jeffrey replied stonily.

Nicole was on her feet. She didn't remember pushing her chair back or standing. "He was *lending* me his *fork*."

Six more bodyguards came out of nowhere and they were all pointing their guns at Thomas, who was lying on his back like a stunned beetle.

"Are you all right?" David asked sharply, peeking around his bodyguard.

She raised her voice. "He was *lending* me his *fork*. Of course I'm all right!"

"Weapons check?" somebody said.

"Clear."

"Perimeter?"

"Clear."

"Code canceled. Comply?"

"Complied."

"Are you well, Highness?" Jeffrey had the nerve to ask, holstering his weapon.

"You big bag of—come with me!"

"Princess—"

"Right *now!*"

"Wait a minute," the king started, but by then she was out of the dining hall.

Jeffrey followed her into the next room, which Nicole saw was a hallway.

"You prick! You did that because he was flirting with me."

"And trying to stab you."

She nearly choked on the urge to punch him in his smug face. "He was not trying to stab me and you know it! You saw us getting cozy, and for whatever weird reason, you didn't like it."

He frowned at her. "Weird reason?"

"You've made it clear you don't want the job, so now . . . what? You're gonna immobilize any decent prospect that comes along?"

He folded his arms across his massive chest and didn't reply.

"Answer me, Jeffrey."

"They're waiting for you at the luncheon. And I need to get back to reassess the threat."

"You're impossible. Try that again and I'll shoot you with your own gun. Now get lost!"

"Princess, I'm currently on duty and—"

"Am I being unclear? Slurring my words? I want you *out of my face*. Go away. *Run* away. What the fuck ever. Just get in the wind, buddy boy, and you can consider *that* a royal command."

She ignored the stricken look on his face. She was completely immune to it. It didn't make her feel bad at all. Nope. Not one bit.

Fuming and heart sore, she went back to the luncheon just in time to hear the king scream, "Well, *somebody* better tell me what the hell is going on!"

"Shut up, Al. Eat your soup."

He pointed his spoon at her, then seemed to think better of it and didn't say anything.

The rest of the conversation was strained, to say the least.

Chapter 31

Jeffrey knocked on the door he had leaned against thousands of times.

"Come!"

He opened it but stayed on the threshold. "You wished to see me, my king?"

"Yeah, come on in, Jeff."

Jeffrey walked into the office. "Majesty?"

"Have a seat, Jeff."

For the first time in his career, Jeffrey took the seat opposite the king. "How may I assist you, my king?"

"You can settle down and unclench. Want a drink? Something to eat?"

"No, sir."

"How about a vacation?"

"No, sir!"

"Calm down, you're so tense you're making me nervous. Granted, your last vacation wasn't much fun—"

"You nearly died. By the time the border patrol eased up enough for me to get back into the country, it was all over."

"—but your last vacation was also four years ago. I think, after what happened at lunch, that you're a little overdue."

"Does the king require my resignation?" he asked stiffly.

"Shit, no!" The king looked honestly stressed, and even worried. Jeffrey had often wished someone would try something on his watch, just so he could have the pleasure of taking a bullet for Alexander Baranov II. And he always felt guilty when he had such thoughts. "I'm just worried about you, Jeff. Nicole popping up out of the woodwork has been stressful for all of us—"

My king, you have no idea.

"—everybody's on edge and—"

She talked to me like she hated me.

"—stressful, sure, and—"

Hated me.

"—a handful, but she's had to adjust to a lot—"

I couldn't bear it if she felt the way she sounded.

"Okay?"

"Of course, my king."

"Okay." King Alexander beamed. "So it's settled. Effective tomorrow, you're on vacation for the rest of the week.

"*What?*"

"Okay, okay, take two weeks. See what a softy I am?"

He cursed himself for not paying more attention. Then he realized: the king was right. He couldn't even focus on orders from the sovereign. What good was he to Nicole in this state?

"That, ah, that won't be necessary, sir. I'll see you Monday morning."

"Take 'er easy, Jeff. Oh, and Jeff! Where's the Dragon right now?"

He consulted his Palm Pilot. "Third floor, north wing. I would guess she's taking more pictures of the family portraits."

"Great. That's fine. Thousand of feet away. Okay. Thanks. Enjoy your time off. You've earned it."

Then why did it feel more like a punishment than a reward?

Chapter 32

Christina Baranov, once Crown Princess of Alaska, now just plain Princess, came at once to answer her daughter's cries.

She cursed Dara's grandfather for letting the almost-four-year-old watch *Lord of the Rings.* This was the third night in a row Dara had dreamed of catapulting severed heads. She soothed her daughter, named for a dead queen, David's mother. And soon enough, the child drifted back to sleep.

David hadn't come to help her. And when David was home, he always came when Dara cried.

Christina was hot tempered, but a good wife who loved her husband beyond all reason, and she said nothing to David when she returned to their bedroom.

"She okay?" David said, not looking away from the television. That in itself was super weird; David never watched television. He never had time. If he wasn't tending the penguins or speaking at an aquarium or studying law or history, he had almost as much paperwork to juggle as Al, or Edmund.

Not anymore.

"Another nightmare about flying severed heads. Remind me to kick your dad's butt up to his shoulder blades tomorrow."

David smiled, clicking rapidly through the channels. "You know he can't refuse her anything."

"He's spoiling her rotten *and* giving her nightmares. The worst of both worlds."

"Don't bug Dad. He's got enough on his mind. Especially after that balls-up of a luncheon."

Shockeroo number eighty-seven, and it had already been a helluva week. David didn't normally talk crude; he left it to her.

She sat on the edge of the bed, trying for noncommittal. "Yeah, I heard Jeffrey had kind of an overreaction. But all those guys are wound so tight I can't believe it hasn't happened before."

"Mmm."

"So how'd it go? Nicole's first official thingamabob?"

"Before or after our gold medalist nearly got concussed?"

"Right. So. Uh. What are you doing?"

"Nothing." Click click click click click. "At all."

"Yeah, uh, we haven't really talked about this."

"Talked about what?"

"How you're suddenly out of the job you've been training for since you were in diapers."

At last, at last he looked at her. "There's nothing to discuss. It's just as much my duty to step aside for the true heir as it was my duty to learn how to—to run things after Dad. You know."

She threw up her hands. "Duty! If I hear that word again this week I'll puke! Fuck duty, how do you *feel?*"

"Fine." Click. Click. Click.

She jerked the remote out of his hand, shut off the television, and tossed the remote across the room.

"Oh," her husband observed, "now that's mature."

"David! Stop being such a damn guy and talk to me! Tell me you're pissed, tell me you're sad, tell me you're thrilled to be off the hook. I don't give a shit, just speak."

Nothing.

"Speak!"

"Arf."

"I hate you," she muttered, getting up from the bed, but he rolled across the mattress, grabbed her arm, and pulled her back down.

"You worship the very ground I walk on and we both know it."

"Don't press your luck."

"Chris, I can't tell you how I feel because I don't know how I feel. I really don't. I'm just—" He groped for words, seemingly at a loss. Or perhaps actually at a loss.

"Well, I don't really care if I'm ever queen. You know that. You always knew that."

"Yes."

"But you've got to have feelings about not being the king."

"I do have feelings." He paused. "I just have no idea what they are."

She understood. She had spent her time as a royal dreading Al's death, dreading the crown. And now that she never had to worry about it again, she wasn't sure if she was relieved or out of sorts. And if she, who'd only been in the royal family a little over four years, didn't know, how could David possibly know?

"You want something? An omelet?" Their suite was the

only one equipped with a kitchen; Christina had been a cook in her old life. "Coddled eggs?"

"I'm sick of eggs. I'd rather have you."

"Oooooh," she said, letting him drag her across the bed and into his lap. "Now if only you had the remote back, you'd be the happiest guy in the country."

Chapter 33

"Uh, hello." Nicole blinked at the stranger standing opposite her door. "Who are you?"

"Natalia Burdenov, Your Highness. I'm new to your detail, effective 0800 today."

Nicole blinked harder. Yesterday had been a disaster—the botched luncheon, her screaming at Jeffrey—complete and total nightmare. She'd spent the rest of the day hiding in a library she'd found. No one had disturbed her, and she'd worked her way through four Hardy Boys books. She had declined to eat with the royal family and had hit the sheets early after someone sent up a sandwich and decaf.

Her favorite sandwich: rare roast beef, mustard, tomatoes, on a sourdough roll.

She wondered how the palace staff ferreted stuff like that out.

Resolved to make a fresh start and hash this thing out with Jeffrey, her plan had been foiled by sleeping late. And now—

"Where's Jeffrey?"

"Off duty for the rest of the week, Your Highness."

She squinted at Natalia, who looked as far from a bodyguard as anyone she'd ever seen: big dark pansy eyes, pale skin, long blond hair in a Valkyrie braid that hung over her left shoulder. Black suit. Armed to the teeth. Sensible flats.

"He's gone?"

"Yes, Highness."

"Did I get him in trouble?"

"No, Highness."

"Would you tell me if I did?"

"Yes, Highness."

Great. They'd assigned her a cyborg.

She sighed. "Well, what's the plan for today, Natalia?"

"You'll be presenting awards to the GSA—"

"What?"

"Girl Scouts of Alaska. Then lunch. Then—"

"Then nothing. I'm off duty then, too."

Natalia didn't blink. Perhaps she hadn't been programmed to. "Yes, Princess."

"And one more thing."

"Yes, Princess?"

"Where's Nicky?"

Chapter 34

After dealing with several giggling preadolescents, all who wanted to know what it was like to be "a real live princess, like Sleeping Beauty!" she made her escape and tracked down the youngest prince. She found him exactly where Natalia had told her he'd be, which was a good trick.

Because when it was just family, the detail left them pretty much alone. They only stuck close at official luncheons and the like. And they were positively leechlike when the royals left the palace grounds. And yet, they always knew where each royal could be found, day or night.

Anyway, Nicky was watching the new Harry Potter movie, which she knew for a fact wouldn't be out in theaters for another six weeks, and munching popcorn in the small theater.

Munching alongside him was Princess Christina.

"Hi, Nicky."

He turned and smiled when he saw her. "Hi, Nicole. Lights!"

The gloomy theater instantly brightened, and the movie shut off.

"Sorry. I didn't mean to interrupt—"

"He's seen it three times already." Christina was studying her with a cool, calculating gaze. "Did you come to rumble? Get payback for that bump on the noggin?"

"Don't flatter yourself."

"To meet your niece?"

"Uh, sorry about that. Sure, but maybe later? I mean, doesn't she have a schedule, too?"

"I'm pretty sure Al is sneaking her Ding-Dongs and ruining her supper," Christina said dolefully. "Why don't you have supper with us? David and me and her, I mean, in our suite? I'll cook."

Oh, right. She had read that Christina Baranov, née Krabbe, had been a cruise line chef before meeting the king, and then David. "Sure, sounds good."

"Are you allergic to anything?"

Amused, Nicole asked, "You don't have paperwork on that?"

"Sure. But who can find it in that haystack?"

"No, no allergies. But I hate green beans."

"Three helpings of *haricots vertes* coming up." Christina tossed another handful of popcorn in her mouth. "So what's on your mind?"

"Actually, Christina, I'm here for him."

"You are? I mean, of course you are." Christina looked surprised. Nicky looked smug. "Listen, I'm sorry about the other day. Even though you started it."

"You really suck at apologies," Nicky told his sister-in-law.

"I'm just saying—no hard feelings, okay?"

"I," Nicole replied, "have no other kind of feelings, on the off chance you hadn't noticed. Now if you don't mind, I'd like to talk to Nicky alone."

"What are you going to do to him?" Christina asked suspiciously, not budging from her seat.

"I'm going to probe his diabolical mind."

"Seriously."

"I am being serious."

Christina turned to the only other blonde in the family. "Do you want me to stay?"

"What for?"

"She's probably got some piano wire on her somewhere. Possibly a crossbow."

"You think I'm in danger because she tried to punch you? *You're* in danger because she tried to punch you. Why don't you go take care of David's penguins or something?"

"You mean it's true?" Nicole said. "There really are penguins living inside the palace? I thought that was an urban legend."

"Don't we all wish." The tall blonde shuddered but got to her feet. "Why don't I go take care of the smelly things? Because I have a life? I'm gonna go make pea soup from scratch."

"Pea soup," Nicky said, shivering. "Why not just vomit into a bowl and call it good?"

"God, you're disgusting." Christina moved up the aisle. "Later, Nicole."

"Maybe."

"Even 'maybe' sounds ominous coming from you." But Christina was talking to herself; Nicole had focused her attention on Nicky.

She sat beside him and said, "If I wanted to find out where a staff member lived while at the same time not making a big deal of it, how would I—"

He handed her a computer printout. It had one name on it, and one address.

Jeffrey Rodinov.

She stared at him. "What are you, a witch? How'd you know what I wanted? How'd you know I'd show up here looking for it?"

"Well, everybody knows Jeffrey was sort of forced into a vacation."

"Forced?" she said sharply. Here she'd been thinking he had gotten himself transferred to another detail, and who could blame him?

"Well, yeah. He's really overdue. It's stressful, watching out for us."

"I can imagine."

"No, Nicole, you can't. Our detail is bored 99.9 percent of the time, and the other tenth of a percent, people are shooting at them—or us—or trying to blow us up."

"I guess I didn't think about it like that." Mostly, she mused, she thought of the detail as grossly invading her privacy as much as they could.

"And he was on Dad's detail for years. That's probably the most stressful detail of all."

"I can imagine."

"No, you can't."

"Okay, okay, we've established I'm the detail dumbass. But you still haven't explained how you can see into the future. Is that your royal superpower?"

"I just figured you'd want to check up on him. Whenever one of our detail is sick or whatever, we usually stop by their place at least once. They're trained to take a bullet or a knife; the least we can do is visit them when they're sick or whatever."

"Okay." Sick or whatever had nothing to do with nothing, but she had no plans to enlighten the Prince of Darkness. "I'm with you so far."

"And I figured you wouldn't know who to ask—Edmund, by the way, when in doubt, always ask Edmund—so I pulled Jeffrey's address out of one of our databases, printed it, and stuck it in my pocket. I figured I'd have to find you, but you tracked me down."

She stared at him. "You're kind of terrifying, you know?"

He arched blond brows at her. "Sure."

"Didn't you blow up the bathrooms at—"

"Nicole!" He grinned. "Don't tell me you believe everything you read."

"Just give me a chance to kill myself if I ever get on your bad side."

"Please. I'm glad you're here. Uh." He colored. "I mean, I'm sorry about your mom and all, but I'm really glad you're here. It's been so *boring* lately."

"Anything to brighten your weird little life." She pocketed the printout. "Thanks for this."

"Please. Next time give me something hard."

"I'll try to stump you."

Chapter 35

Jeffrey sat in his living room, drinking Scotch.

This was a horrible idea, for several reasons.

One: He didn't drink.

Two: If he did drink, it wouldn't be Scotch, which tasted like rubbing alcohol to him, no matter how good or how old. And this had been a Christmas gift from the king; he knew it went for at least three hundred bucks. Still, it tasted like a doctor's office.

Three: At the rate he was going, he was looking at a real bitch kitty of a hangover tomorrow.

And four: It wasn't helping. He was still ashamed, and horny, and mad.

He drained the glass.

At least Nicole was in good hands. Natalia may have been the youngest agent on the detail, but what she lacked in experience she made up for in cold-blooded efficiency. And she had been an Olympian-level sharpshooter. Quite a catch for the detail and an impeccable military background, too.

But, oh God, he wished he was the one watching out for Nicole. Who knew what mischief that mouthy, gorgeous, irritating princess would get up to? For that matter, who knew what—

There was a tap on the door.

Jeffrey cursed. That would be a palace rep, asking him to return to duty for whatever reason. Except he couldn't, because he'd been drinking.

He got to his feet and walked to the door, stooping to look through the peephole.

"Oh my God!" He yanked the door open. "Tell me Natalia knows where you are."

Nicole brushed past him. "Natalia of the Borg thinks I'm asleep in my bed. Jeez, nice fumes, did you fall into a brewery on your way home?"

"Nicole!" he howled.

"Please come in, Nicole. So nice to see you again, Nicole."

"Nicole! Sneaking out to walk around the palace property is one thing. But you can't leave the palace proper, for God's sake!" He fought the urge to gouge out his own eyes in horror. "The detail is going to *shit*."

"Only if you rat me out." She was looking around his slightly messy apartment with interest. "So this is where you live when you're not driving me crazy."

"I drive *you* crazy?" He tried to drink more Scotch but realized anew that the glass was empty. "That's funny, that's hilarious, I would have bet large amounts of currency that it was the other way around."

"Nice place."

"Thanks." He tried to see it through her eyes: the living room comfortably furnished with an oversized chair and a sectional couch. The fireplace. The kitchen, with dinner dishes still stacked in the sink. A serviceable bathroom with an extra-large whirlpool tub; he got kinks in his back and neck from being alert every moment of every hour he was on the job, and the tub did wonders for his muscles.

And the—the—

"Nicole, what are you doing here?"

"Well." She shrugged out of her jacket and tossed it over the back of the couch. "You're off duty for the rest of the week. And I'm off the grounds. So I figured, what better time for us to have sex than now? You're not a bodyguard. And I'm not a princess."

Clearly, the stress of palace living had driven her insane, poor girl. "Of course you're a princess, how could you ever not be a—"

"I'll rephrase. I don't feel it here." She lightly touched her left breast and he clutched the glass so hard he thought it would break. "People can 'Her Highness' me until they pass out, but it doesn't feel real. None of this feels real."

"You have to give it time. More time than a week. Like it or not, you're a princess born. You don't have to feel it. You just are."

"Nice speech."

"Thank you."

"No, seriously. I'm all tingly and stuff."

Then, incredibly, she was stripping her T-shirt over her head. "Okay, that wasn't quite true," she went on conversationally. "You feel real. I think about you all the time. And we'll never have a better chance than this one." She was shucking out of her jeans.

"Please stop undressing!" he croaked.

"I was kind of hoping you would *start* undressing."

"Nicole—I—your father would shoot me with my own gun. And then several of his."

"Aren't we a little old to worry about what Daddy thinks?"

"But I—you—we—I—"

"Oh." She blushed to her eyebrows. "You don't want to. Oh, boy." She covered her eyes. "I don't normally misread a situation this badly. I don't suppose you've got a bottomless pit I can throw myself into."

Silence.

"Jeffrey?"

Then she felt his hands on her wrists, pulling her fingers away from her face. He had moved with that silently, spooky speed.

And then, oh thank God, he was kissing her and yanking at the buttons on his shirt.

Chapter 36

She tried to help him with his shirt, but he was in a hurry and it tore. She hadn't realized a good quality men's shirt could rip like a Kleenex. She fumbled at his belt and, oh boy, was there a sexier sound than a man's belt coming undone?

He yanked at his pants and they staggered back and forth while he tried not to trip, and finally he kicked free of them. Then he was pushing her bra cups down and sucking greedily at her nipples.

She arched against him and groaned, "Feels like you're doing that between my legs."

"Wait," he said, voice muffled against her flesh.

She did what she had wanted to do for days: plunged her fingers into his black, curly hair, stroking, touching. His hair was coarse and soft at the same time, crackling beneath her fingers like a cat's fur.

He fumbled for the middle of her back, fumbled more, then muttered, "Fuck it," and yanked. She grinned as he relieved her of her (now useless) bra.

"You know, those hook and eye things are a pain to get back into—"

"Nicole, hush."

"House rules, huh?"

"Something like that." He scooped her up in his arms and practically ran to what she hoped was a bedroom.

And . . . it was! He dropped her on the bed and pulled down his boxers. She wriggled out of her panties, trying not to stare at him. His chest was furred with dark hair, tapering down his stomach and into his pubic hair. His sex jutted out at her and she could see how the tip gleamed.

Now she was *really* trying not to stare. Although why she was surprised, she didn't know. Why wouldn't a guy with big hands and broad shoulders be big . . . in all ways?

She was so busy trying not to stare at him, she didn't realize he was staring at her. "Oh my God," he breathed. "You look—"

"Bloated?" she suggested. "My monthly visitor is due in four or five days."

He considered for a moment. "Incredibly, that did not ruin the mood. And the word I had in mind was beautiful."

"Come here."

He obliged, which was very fine. She couldn't get enough of his mouth, she felt like devouring him. Then he trailed kisses down her breasts, lingered on her nipples, then moved to her stomach. He put his hands on her knees and slowly spread her legs; then he was kissing her where she had longed to be kissed.

"Oh God!"

He was parting her lower lips with his tongue again and again, teasing and licking and kissing. She pumped her hips against his mouth in pure unconscious reaction, and then he was—oh he was—he was fucking her with his tongue.

"Please *please* get up here!"

He obliged and kissed her hard. He tasted like salt and fresh grass and her. She heard the bedside table drawer slide open and realized he was finding a condom by touch while kissing her so hard she was having trouble finding her breath.

She broke the kiss and said, “Let me.” She ripped the corner of the foil with her teeth, pulled out the condom, and grabbed his stiff dick. He shuddered like a horse and she eased her grip, then rolled the condom on.

He fell upon her like a starving animal, slid into her up to the hilt with no further formalities, and she wrapped her legs around his hips and pumped back at him stroke for stroke.

They surged together, kissing and scratching and writhing, and she was astonished to feel her orgasm closing in on her. It normally took quite a bit longer.

“Dry spell’s over,” she gasped, and in reply he pressed his face to her neck and thrust harder.

Then she was flying—or, at least, it always seemed like that to her. Flying and free and soaring and going wherever she wanted to go.

“Jeffrey,” she whispered, still feeling the internal quakes.

“Nicole.”

“Do it again.”

For reply he took a deep breath and she realized he was breathing in the scent of her hair, and the thought of such tenderness from a man who looked like a brute was all it took; she fell over the edge again, swooping and soaring.

Then he was stiffening in her arms, and then she slowly settled back to the planet.

Chapter 37

"No. No! No damned way!"

"Aw. Don't be like that, Big Al."

"Out! I mean it! The detail has orders to shoot to kill."

"It's nice to feel wanted."

He gave her the scowl that sent most people scurrying for cover, but that just made her grin widen. "Bad enough I have to put up with you during the course of my business day. But I refuse—*refuse*—to put up with you during my own time."

"But you're in your office."

"News flash, Dragon: I can be in any of these rooms I want. It's my fucking house. Plus, this is my time off."

"Not so, Big Al. Kings don't get time off. Neither do their biographers, and let me tall ya, that's something they didn't mention in grad school. What're you doing, anyhow?"

"Looking up porn on the Internet."

"Haw! Like you don't have a battalion of underlings to fetch you all the porn you want. C'mon, you know I'll drag it out of you after a while. Cough up, big guy. Watcha doing?"

"Reading Nicole's scripts."

"Really?" She came around the desk and peeked at his

laptop. Today's suit was navy blue; the shoes were red Keds. He got a whiff of—cookies?—when she bent over to look.

"*Die Hard: Enough Is Enough,*" she read aloud. "She wrote this?"

"Rewrote. It's her—it was her other job. Punching up scripts for Hollywood."

"How many d'you find so far?"

"Twenty-eight."

"That's nice work, if you can get it. Hollywood's got the bucks t'spare." Her hand was resting on his shoulder; he doubted she realized. Her soft, slim hand. The hand of a scholar. His hands were too big, too blocky, and riddled with calluses. "I still can't believe she didn't skedaddle for L.A. when the shitstorm began."

"Because she's a Baranov," he said simply. "We don't run."

The Dragon was now drumming her fingers on his shoulder. "That's of historical significance, doncha know."

"Not running."

"Well, yeah. But the other, too. We've had royal poets and royal songwriters, but never a royal script writer."

"You're a plague on me, not her."

"Well now, that's true enough, Big Al." She was staring down at him. Her curls framed her face in a dark red cloud. "I guess I can wait until you kick it before being a plague on her."

"Yeah, well, the way this month is going, that's gonna happen sooner rather than later."

"Now that," she said, taking off her glasses, "would be a pure d-shame."

And then she leaned down and kissed him softly on the mouth.

Chapter 38

The Dragon, well used to being tossed out of the king's office, took the whole thing with her usual equanimity. The important thing was, she had finally done what she'd fantasized about for the past three years.

Al was gonna be a tough nut to crack. Scuttlebutt had it he was still in love with the late, treacherous Queen Dara. But she was a historian, and took the long view. He'd come around eventually.

Besides, who'd be able to refuse a chance at her? She was smart, she was sexy, she had the ass of a twenty-five-year-old.

Hmm. Perhaps she was getting a little obsessed with her own ass. Something for her shrink to work on; they could forget about her traumatizing freshmen year of college for a while.

"No, no, no," Al had said, escorting her out of his office with a firm hand in the middle of her back. "We're not doing this."

She tried to drag her feet, but the sucker was as strong as he was big. "Why the hell not, Big Al?"

"Because it'd be like the Road Runner doing the Coyote.

A crime against all the laws of nature. Also, you're fired again."

Then the detail drove her back to her hotel.

"You're mine, Big Al," she said aloud, chowing down on fairly awful barbecued ribs. Why she bought BBQ North of Missouri she didn't know. *The Daily Show* was on—fake history! Hurrah!—and she was sitting cross-legged in her lonely bed.

Did the big oaf think she kept coming back to write his memoirs, for the luvva Pete? She'd been gone the day she met him. Big, gruff, great-looking, with the energy of a man half his age and the vocabulary of a sailor. She'd been gone at that moment; her love only deepened with each firing.

Because the Dragon was tired of being alone.

And Big Al was, too. Poor sucker just didn't know it.

"It's only a matter of time."

Then she ordered another platter from room service. Scheming always made her hungry.

Chapter 39

"Nicole?"

"Mmmmm?"

"You have to go."

She stretched, then curled back against him like a sleepy kitten. "Too tired."

He stroked her hair, running his fingers through the silky strands. He was still having trouble digesting the events of the past forty minutes.

Nicole—the Princess—had snuck out. Again. Had come to him. Tried to persuade him to the absurd notion that this week she wasn't royalty and he wasn't a bodyguard. And then she'd—and then he'd—

But she was still here. And that was a problem.

No, it wasn't.

Yes, it was.

"Nicole." He shook her gently. "You have to get dressed. I have to take you back. If they notice you're gone, everyone will go right out of their minds."

She yawned, rolled over, and stroked his penis, which went from sleepy to extremely interested in about two seconds. "So? Oh, hey, is this for me?"

He gritted his teeth and pulled away from her. "You'd frighten your family just to get laid again?"

She jerked away from him and sat up. "They don't feel like my family," she said sullenly. "My mother was my family. My father was just a two-week party for her."

"Even so." He rose, strapped on his wristwatch, then walked around the room gathering the clothes that hadn't been ruined. "Get dressed."

"That's it? You fuck me—"

"I think you fucked me."

"—and then kick me out? Jeffrey, your pillow talk *sucks*." "Sucks" was punctuated as she hurled a pillow at his chest.

"You have to go back," he said stonily, ignoring the inner voice that begged to differ. Ignoring the urge to take her back to bed and never, ever let her go. "Right now. We're done talking about it."

"Damn right we are," she hissed, and climbed out of his bed.

He tried to help her with her clothes, but she slapped his hands away and nearly burned his eyes out of his skull with the force of her glare.

He drove her back, his heart growing heavier the closer they got to the palace. She was fuming in the passenger seat, arms folded over her chest, scowling at the road.

He got her as close as he could to her suite without actually driving across the lawn. As she got out, he leaned over and said, "Don't do this again, Nicole."

"Don't . . . *worry!*" "Worry" was punctuated with the door slamming.

He rested his head on the steering wheel, and it was a good five minutes before he could turn the car around.

Chapter 40

Nicole found her way into the palace via a little-used servants' entrance. Oh, Nicky's digital map had been a godsend. She was able to slip inside and make it back to her suite in fifteen minutes.

Where an astonished Natalia watched her approach her own closed door. "Your Highness! I didn't—what are you—how did you—?"

"Some things," she said, her body still tingling from Jeffrey's urgent touch, "will never be told."

"But how did you—"

"Good night, Natalia."

The blonde bowed. "Highness."

Nicole shut the door behind her, taking in the three-room suite at a glance. Private bathroom, sitting room decorated in shades of gold and red, deluxe bedroom decorated in gold and blue. Stuffed with furniture so old and expensive she was afraid to use any of it.

Except the bed. The bed might be an antique four poster, too, but it was sturdy enough. And a good thing, too, because she had every intention of throwing herself on it and crying for an hour or so.

Chapter 41

Exhausted from a sleepless night and too tired for breakfast, Nicole staggered into the hall outside her room.

Natalia bowed. "Good morning, Your Highness."

"Oh, God. Cof—" Natalia was already handing her a cup. "Natalia, whoever programmed you did a helluva job."

Natalia didn't twitch. "Yes, Highness. The king would like to see you, Highness."

"I gotta see the king? Now? Great. I have no friggin' idea how to get there from here."

"*You* don't, Highness?"

Nicole stared at her bodyguard suspiciously. Natalia didn't blink. In fact, Nicole's eyes were watering with sympathy as the seconds ticked by and Natalia still didn't blink. "You got something on your mind, Natalia?"

"Certainly not, Highness."

"Well, super. You mind walking me over there?"

"Not at all, Highness." The blonde tapped her earpiece. "Hunter to see Warrior."

"How too fucking G.I. Joe," she muttered.

"Thank you, Highness."

A few minutes later, they were in the hallway outside the

king's office. She was pretty sure. All the damn hallways looked the same to her.

A man she'd never seen was leaning on the wall, arms crossed, but he stood straight and tall when she approached, then bowed.

"Hi."

"Your Highness."

"I'm supposed to talk to the king."

"Yes, Princess Nicole, he's expecting you."

"Handing off Hunter," Natalia said with cool formality.

"Acknowledged. Go get an early lunch, Natty."

"Sir. Highness."

"Handing off?" she asked the man. He sure didn't look like a bodyguard: slim, shorter than she was, soberly dressed, small hands. He looked like he was Edmund's assistant or something. "What am I, a relay baton?"

He smiled. "Hardly, Princess." He touched his index finger to the corner of his left eyebrow. "Have a nice day."

She rapped on the door with her knuckles and at the harried, "Come in, quick!" opened the door and walked in.

The king was on his feet, staring anxiously over her shoulder. "Are you alone? Is she out there?"

"Yes. Who?"

"The Dragon! I know she's lurking around here somewhere, just waiting to—never mind."

"Well, she isn't lurking in the corridor. Are you okay? You look a little stressed."

"Stressed," he mumbled, "is not the word. You're sure nobody's out there?"

"Just some guy I never saw before. What can I do for you, Al?"

"Aw, come on, kiddo." He slumped back into his chair. "Is 'Dad' so hard? Pop? Papa?"

She yawned and sat across from him. "Is that why you called me up here?"

"No, you look like shit."

"Is *that* why—"

"Naw, naw." He waved away her irritation. "Just an early morning observation."

"Well, thanks so much. You're not exactly looking your best, either."

"I'm in the best shape of any one of you guys," the king bragged.

"You'd have to be," she admitted, "to run this funny farm."

"If you're having trouble sleeping, maybe you should see Doc Hedman. Alexandria was having terrible insomnia a couple years ago and he was able to help her out. This was before she got married to Sheldon."

"That's it!" she cried, and was surprised when the king flinched. She didn't think he *could* flinch. "Sheldon Rivers. That's the American who married Alexandria. She's with him now, right? At some aquarium or whatever?"

"Yeah, and he didn't marry her, she married him."

"You say tomato, I say toe-maw-toe. Anyway, it was driving me nuts, trying to remember another relative's name. You're a big bunch to keep track of."

"What can I say, I'm a fertile son of a bitch."

She covered her eyes. "Please, Al. I'm begging you. We're headed for overshare country."

He laughed. He had a great laugh, booming and kingly. She looked up at him and smiled in spite of herself. Then took a closer look and lost her smile. "You look more than a little stressed. Is everything all right?"

"No, but it's nothing for you to worry about. I called you up here for two things—thanks for coming so quickly, by the way. Thing one, how are you doing? Do you need anything? To put it another way—"

"Thanks, because English is my ninth language."

"—shaddup—are you not getting something you need?"

"The food's great, everybody's nice, I don't need anything."

"Because speaking of Sheldon, you might want to talk to him. The last thing that guy ever wanted was to be a prince. But he sucked it up. And you think Christina wanted to be the Queen of Alaska? Ever? You could learn a lot from those two weirdos."

"Thanks. I'll keep it in mind." She sipped her coffee.

"We were, ah, surprised when you didn't dine with us."

"I needed some time alone." In fact, she'd skipped the dinner with Christina, too, and felt horribly guilty. Well, she'd track her down today and apologize.

She leaned forward, rattled by the hurt look in his eyes. That's all she seemed to do these days: hurt the men in her life. "You gotta try to understand, Al. It was me and mom, and then it was me. I fish and hunt for a living. I like the quiet. I love the solitude. And here, I don't have either. I didn't think it was possible to feel claustrophobic in here, but I do. I really do."

"Sweetie, how can we do better?"

"That's a nice offer, but it's me, not you guys. I'm the one who has to adjust. I'm the one who has to change. I wouldn't have sat for the DNA test if I wasn't reconciled to that. And none of it's your fault."

"It could be argued that all of it's my fault." She opened her mouth, but he rushed forward. "Nicole, I friggin' hate seeing you unhappy."

"Well, it's not much fun on this end, either." But she took the sting out of her words with a small grin. "You said you had two reasons."

"Yeah, you've really got a gift. I've been reading some of the scripts you've—"

"No!" she practically screamed. Al reared back in his chair. "Oh, God, tell me, *tell me* you didn't read any of the dreck I wrote for Hollywood."

"But you saved a bunch of movies! *Killing Cardinals* had a totally different, sucky ending according to the trades. And you single-handedly rescued the dialogue for *I'm Okay, You're Insane.*"

"It's just to pay the bills, Al. It's not art."

"Well, I thought it was pretty nifty, swifty."

"God, the humiliation never stops around here, does it?"

"Guess not. You know, if you ever thought about writing a book . . ."

A book. A fishing guide. Her mother's story. *Her* story. Sure, she'd thought about it. But who had the time?

"You're not implying I'd have all this leisure time to write, are you?"

"I'm just saying. If it's something you wanted to do, there's not much in your way. It's not like you have to spend your creativity fixing other people's words. Not anymore."

She raised her eyebrows. "That's . . . an interesting perspective."

"I got tons of perspective," he bragged. "I got it running out of me like . . . stuff that runs out of me. By the way, three American movie studios have called here looking for you. They want to buy the rights to your story."

"Oh, sure. When I was a lonely hack they wouldn't return my calls. Now they want to toss money at me and make a movie out of my life. Pass." She rose from her seat. "Still, you've given me something to think about."

"I'm good at shit like that," he said, lacing his fingers beside his head. "G'wan, get out of here."

"Later, Al."

"Wait!" He was leaning forward in his chair and looking anxious. "Look first and tell me; is the Dragon out there?"

Nicole opened the door and checked both ends of the corridor, waving to the short bodyguard. Then she went back inside. "Coast is clear."

"Great. I'm dying for some scrambled eggs. Had a conference call so I didn't eat with the kids today."

"Well." She took a deep breath. "I haven't eaten yet. We could eat together. Unless it's a working breakfast or—"

"No no no! It's not a working breakfast. Yeah, that'd be great. Come on, I'll show you one of the prettiest rooms in the palace."

"Don't you have to sign bills into law or something?"

"Fuck it."

"You're an inspiration to us all," she said dryly. "I assume this means that when I'm queen, I can constantly blow off my work."

"What do I care? I'll be worm food by then. Come on, let's get out of here before Edmund brings me more work."

"That bastard," she agreed, and followed him out the door.

Chapter 42

The king watched Nicole pick at her eggs and ham, and drink cup after cup of black coffee. Something was wrong, and he didn't think it was just the events of her birthright coming to light.

No, it was something else.

"If you don't like the eggs, we can get you something else."

She forced a smile. "I'm just not very hungry, I guess."

"Still, you gotta eat."

"You were right," she replied, obviously anxious to change the subject. "This is the prettiest room in the palace."

"This" was a solarium on the east side, second floor. The entire east wall was one big window. It was warm in there even in the middle of January. It was one of the few rooms that didn't have a fireplace. Thanks to the greenhouse effect, it didn't need one.

"Yup. Used to do my homework in here when I was a kid."

"It's hard to picture you as a little boy," she teased. "I bet you were more of a handful than Nicky is."

Al groaned. "That kid is the punishment for all my sins. Karma's a bitch, y'know?"

"You should write greeting cards. That's quite a poetic touch."

"Hey, we can't all be professional writers-for-hire."

"Mmm. Speaking of writers, what'd the Dragon do to freak you out? And didn't you fire her?"

"I've fired her eleven times," he said gloomily, still running hot and cold every time he remembered her mouth on his, her hands pressing his shoulders, her skirt riding up as she sat in his lap. "She keeps coming back."

"Yeah, but you could make her stay away if you really wanted to."

"Yeah, I—I suppose."

"She likes you, you know."

He stared at her.

She shrugged and forked up some egg. "Just sayin'."

"I'm her project, not her—her—"

"Sorry, Al, I'm calling bullshit. You think she keeps coming back for the privilege of writing down your old war stories?"

"It doesn't matter. We're not talking about this. Besides, I—in my heart, I'm still married."

"Queen Dara."

"Yes."

"Do you—did you love her?"

"She was the first person I loved more than myself. And then she gave me amazing children. Even if I hated her, I'd honor her for that alone."

"But, Al. It's been so long. Fifteen years or so, right?"

"Give or take," he admitted.

"Why do you want to be alone?"

"Why do you?"

He could see he'd shocked her with the observation. She

stammered for a few seconds, then said, "It's not the same thing."

"It's not?" he asked quietly.

"You can get married again. But in my whole life, I'll only have one mother." She bowed her head. "She knew me better than anyone. She could have gotten me through this. I'd give everything I had, and everything you have, just to talk to her one more time."

"Nicole—honey—"

"Oh, God, I just miss her so much!" she cried, and sobbed into her hands.

Al was out of his seat in half a second, patting her on the shoulder. "Nicole, honey, it gets easier, I promise it does. Not just adjusting to us. The grief. It won't always be a killing thing. I swear to you, you'll miss her forever, but eventually you'll only think of the good, never the bad."

She leaned against his hip. "It's just so hard, Dad. I didn't think it would be so hard."

So he comforted her, as he had comforted the tears of all his children. And though Nicole never remembered the first time she called him Dad, the king never forgot.

Chapter 43

"*There* you are, Big Al!"

The king's hands jerked. Papers flew. "Gaaahhh!" he screamed.

"Don't scream, my king, we only just got your office door fixed," Edmund begged. He turned. "Good morning, Ms. Bragon. No, no, everything's fine," he told the out-of-breath bodyguard. "Thank you very much." He shut the door. "Something to drink, Ms. Bragon? Coffee? Juice?"

"I'll just drink in the sight of the glorious king of Alaska, if y'all don't mind."

Al rested his head on his desk.

"I don't mind," Edmund admitted, "but frankly I can't imagine anyone being that thirsty. I'll leave you to your work, ma'am. Sir."

"Yeah, you do that, Edmund darlin'." The door closed behind Edmund and the Dragon grinned down at him. "Ain't you glad to see me?"

His head jerked up off his desk and he scowled. "Hell, no! You're fired. And banned! And fired. Go away or I'll yell rape."

"You'd never." She plopped down in her usual seat. "I can't believe you're passing up the incredible opportunity

I'm throwing in your kingly lap. You out of your mind, boy?"

"I haven't been a boy since I was four. And complications like that, I do not need. Besides, I have to focus on Nicole. And David! Poor kid's out of a job and he doesn't know whether to shit or go blind. And Nicky. He's been way too quiet lately; I don't trust that budding psychopath. And—"

"Sounds like you're takin' care of ever'body, Al. 'Cept yourself, o'course."

"Spare me your hideous brand of psychology."

"Okey-dokey. How about I just plant another smacker on that kingly snoot?"

He actually cringed back. Her grin widened. Oh, this was gonna be *fun*. She'd held her feelings in for three years before realizing that was no way to catch the King of Alaska. Now he was going to pay for every soulful look she'd given him, every natural impulse she'd squashed, every time she'd betrayed her feelings.

"Please don't molest me again," he begged. "I can't take any more this week. I absolutely can't."

"Then tell me about Nicole's mama."

"That's blackmail, you horrible horrible thing!"

"A-yup. It's also called getting the job done." Impersonal as a secretary, she took out her notebook. "So, talk. You're s'posed to be getting married. You take off. You go to a bar and order a drink. Or maybe your detail does. Either way, you meet the bartender. And . . ."

"And none of your damn business!"

"Did you put your big, smelly, fishy hands all over her boobs and make her moan like a donkey?"

"Stop it, stop it!" he screamed.

"Did you hit her with the old 'hey, baby, mind if I knock you up with an illegitimate daughter' line?"

He was actually banging his head on the desk. "Hate you. Hate you. Hate you."

"Haw! You love me, Big Al. You just won't admit it. Anyway, back to Nicole's conception. When the condom broke, did you pretend you'd had a vasectomy? Or did you just—"

"Die! Die, die!"

She jotted it all down and managed to needle him for another ten minutes before he gave up and threw her out.

Chapter 44

"Damn, Christina, you can *cook*! Here all I thought you were good for was throwing sucker punches."

Christina, who had been starting to smile, changed tactics and frowned. Dara gurgled with joy as she watched the play of emotions on her mother's face.

"Eat your applesauce," she told her daughter. To Nicole, "F-U-C-K Y-O-U-R-S-E-L-F."

"Mama, what's fook yr lelf?"

"Never mind. Eat."

"I told you," David said, not bothering to hold back his laughter, "she's already starting to read. Spelling out your colorful vocabulary will work for maybe another six months."

"I can see all the parent–teacher conferences now," Nicole teased. She forked in more linguine with clams—clams that had been in the ocean that very morning—and chased it with a glass of milk. "Your Highness, the littlest Highness called me a B-I-T-C-H today, and while I'm obliged to obey her, I feel she—"

"Oh, just stop," Christina groaned, sitting back down. "You're giving me a migraine."

"Then my job here is done. Seriously, this is the best pasta I've ever had."

Christina and David waited for the follow-up insult.

"No, really. That's all I was gonna say."

"Oh. Thank you."

"Thank you!" Dara sang, big blue eyes gleaming, applesauce drooling down her chin. She blotted it with her own napkin. "N'cole, are you going to live here forever?"

"I'm afraid so. I'm trapped, just like you."

"We all are," David assured her.

"Hooray!"

"Ow. Dara, you've got your mother's lungs but, fortunately, your father's intelligence."

"Why did I invite her to dinner?" the princess asked the prince.

"Because essentially, you're a good person."

Christina sighed. "I was afraid that was why."

Chapter 45

At ten o'clock that night came the long-awaited knock on his door.

Jeffrey didn't get up to answer it. "Go back to the palace, Nicole!"

More knocking.

"I'm not letting you in, Nicole!"

Insistent pounding. He ignored it and sipped his milk. No Scotch tonight, by God. Once this week was enough. She'd eventually take the hint and go away. Find another lover. And he didn't care. Not even remotely.

The knocking stopped and he gritted his teeth so he wouldn't leap out of his chair, kick his own door down, haul her into his apartment by the hair, and do her on the living room carpet.

It had been a mistake. And he never made the same mistake twice. No matter how delectable. No matter how softly she moaned his name in his ear. No matter how—

No matter.

He had decided she had taken the hint when the car battery crashed through the sliding glass doors leading to the back lawn.

"Hello," Nicole said cheerfully, picking her way through

the broken glass. "Did you know your neighbors have the most interesting garbage? I don't think you're supposed to put those in the garbage."

"Freeze!" he roared, and she froze. Then he set down his milk glass, crunched across the glass, picked her up in his arms, and carried her to the glass-free zone. Then he set her down. Or tried to. The trouble was, she'd been kissing his ear while he carried her, and the throbbing between his legs told him he had about five seconds before he gave up the battle.

"Nicole, I never make the same—"

"I had to take care of myself with my fingers this morning," she whispered into the ear she'd been kissing. "That's how much I missed you."

He ran with her into the bedroom.

Chapter 46

They didn't make it as far as the bed. They made it as far as the hallway. Then he lowered her to the carpet and commenced yanking her clothes off.

Nicole did her best to help, and supposed she should be frightened by his urgency, but the truth was, it thrilled her, warmed her to her toes and—and other places. It kindled her own lust, made her feel closer to him, closer to him than she had been with anybody. She'd had one-night stands. In college she had dated the same guy for a year and a half. In her twenties, the occasional dalliance or relationship doomed to fail.

But all of it together couldn't equal the passion the two of them were generating in a cramped, dark hallway on a first-floor apartment in Juneau, Alaska, twenty two miles from her ancestral home.

He pulled. She tugged. He yanked. She pressed. He kissed her again and again, her eyes, her throat, her breasts. She begged. He shoved. Then he was inside her, sliding in with sweet, delicious friction, and she came almost at once, bucking and jerking against him; then he was shuddering over her, and then he collapsed on top of her.

"Ulf," she managed, before his weight drove all the air

out of her lungs. Quietly suffocating, she beat him on the shoulder until he rolled off her with a groan. "Oh, sweet Jesus! I can breathe again!"

"Shut up," he growled.

"Isn't that 'shut up, Your Highness'?" she teased.

"Not in my apartment. Here, it's Nicole."

"Finally, he unclenches!"

"Also, if you take another lover, I'll kill him, then you, then myself."

"How sweet!"

He pressed his palms to his eyes. She could see the sweat gleaming on his body, could smell his good clean smell, and wanted him all over again.

"What is it?"

"I don't know if I hate you or love you."

"Aw." She snuggled against him. "Can't you do both?"

Chapter 47

"Big Al! Where you been hiding all day?"

Holly had to stifle a laugh as she saw the Alaskan monarch flinch away from her. It felt like she'd been prowling around the palace half the night. The detail didn't tell her shit; they viewed her as some sort of extra-annoying reporter.

"Get lost," Al said rudely. "I got enough on my plate without you getting even more annoying. Which I didn't think was possible, until this morning."

"Rack 'em up," she told him. "Bowling's no fun for just one."

So he did. And then he beat her ass so badly at bowling she fumed for ten minutes before challenging him to a rematch.

"Holly."

"Not now, Big Al, I'm lining up a split that will humiliate the Alaskan monarchy until the end of time." She was holding up her bright purple bowling ball and measuring the distance. She let fly and knew the second the ball left her hand that it was good. She jumped up and down as the last four pins went over with a clatter, giving her the game.

"Boo-ya! *That's* what a good ole Texas whuppin' feels like, Big Al."

"Don't remind me," he said sullenly, marking down the score.

"That's one for you and one for me."

"Thanks, I can count."

"You wanna go for the tie breaker? U. S. of A. versus Alaska, winner take all?"

He brightened. "What are the stakes?"

"Wellllll . . . tell you what. I win, I get to take you to bed."

He reddened, but his blue eyes narrowed and he studied her with a look she had seen a thousand times from men of all ages. "And what do I get if I win?"

"Why, the very same thing!"

He threw his head back and laughed. She loved his laugh. Finally, he was able to choke it off and said, "It'll never work, Holly."

"Don't know 'til you try, ain't that so?"

"But, Holly, I hate you with every molecule in my body."

"That's why there's all them sparks between us."

"Sparks? That's one word for it. Germs is what I was thinking."

"Big Al, you know you can't hold me off forever. A man like you has needs."

"That's what I always say! But the kids always tell me to shush up."

"They don't see you like I do, Big Al. And thank goodness."

He rested a finger on her nose. He leaned in and whispered, "Did you know your accent gets thicker when you're nervous?"

"Nuh-uh, does not. I'm from Texas; nothin' has scared us since the Alamo."

"Is that right?"

"Bet your royal ass."

"Holly, the queen and I—our relationship was very complicated. And I owe the mother of my children some—"

"The queen is dead," Holly said. "Long live me. Now rack 'em up."

Chapter 48

Edmund Dante smoothed his perfectly smooth suit jacket, patted his unmussed hair, flicked imaginary lint off his shoulder, then left his rooms and strolled toward the west kitchens.

He courteously greeted every staff member by name and received battalions of "Good morning, Mr. Dante," and "Hi, Edmund," and "Good morning, sir," greetings as he went. He stopped one of the chambermaids, fresh from maternity leave, and asked after the baby. He stopped one of Prince Alexander's footmen and asked how his ailing mother was doing.

He knew everyone. He knew everything. The smallest detail did not escape him. All was right with the world.

After observing the kitchen staff for a minute, it was obvious there had been no last-minute disasters and breakfast would be served on time, which today meant 8:00 A.M. That gave him an hour and a half to read everyone's schedules, wake the king, and be debriefed by the detail.

Yes, it would be close.

He turned to leave, only to hear, "Edmund!"

He turned back, and deftly caught the orange one of the

cooks had tossed him. "Put it in your pocket for luck," she said, smiling. "Knowing you, it's all you'll eat today."

"Thank you, Carrie. And good morning."

He found his way to the king's chambers, picking up the schedules from his office on the way. Nothing out of the ordinary here, either, and that was very well. In fact, a refreshing change—no outside visitors, except for Miss Holly Call-Me-Dragon. Ah, poor King Alexander. She was his cross to bear.

"Good morning, Mr. Dante."

"Good morning, Mr. Reynolds. All well, I trust."

"A quiet night," Reynolds replied. He looked exceptionally cheerful for a normally stone-faced detail man. "For the most part."

"Oh? Glad to hear it."

"Yes, sir. Quiet. For the most part."

"Mr. Reynolds, are you quite all right?"

"Quite, Mr. Dante." Reynolds fished out his two-way. "Bookman to see Warrior."

"May I have your permission to enter, Mr. Reynolds?" Not that he needed it. There wasn't a single room in the palace off limits to him; he had played here as a child and they all knew it. Still, the courtesies must be observed. That was no surprise, either.

"Yes, sir."

Edmund sighed with satisfaction. No surprises. A place for everything and everything in its place. The sun rose in the east and set in the west. The schedules were constantly updated but always correct.

He rapped twice and opened the door.

And froze.

And did something he had never done in the service of his king: He shouted, "Oh my God, what are you two *doing?*"

Chapter 49

Natalia was new to the detail and wasn't sure she liked it. Granted, it was the highest honor offered by the Alaskan military. And granted, she had worked hard to get here.

But her charge, Princess Nicole, was sneaking out at night. The king had, inexplicably, begun sleeping with the Dragon. Jeffrey, the detail's rock, was on vacation.

And the woman in charge of Christina's detail confided that she suspected the Crown Princess was pregnant. Like any of them wanted to go on *that* wild ride again. She hadn't been there at the time, but she'd heard all the rumors.

The detail was famous for it; one man's gossip was another woman's way to better protect her charge.

Now here came Mr. Dante, looking—say it isn't so—rattled.

"Natalia."

"Sir."

"The king—the king—"

"Has there been a schedule update, sir?" she asked, playing dumb.

"Damn right there has!" the man nearly screamed, then got hold of himself. "Forgive me. I—I haven't had breakfast yet. My blood sugar is low."

"You might try eating that orange in your pocket," she said helpfully.

"Yes, I might. Is the princess in?"

And that was the sticky spot. Because she had no idea whether Nicole was in there or not. She hadn't heard her leave. But she never did. And Nicole hadn't come past her to get back in. It was shameful to be ready to open a door and have no idea whether her charge was in there or not.

"I . . . think so."

The sweaty, stressed Edmund started to snap a response, then took a deep breath. "Natalia, please don't worry. The princess can take care of herself, as she has demonstrated again and again. And she's sneaking off to visit Jeff. So even when you don't know where she is, she's in good hands."

Natalia felt her mouth pop open in surprise and almost broke Rule Number One with a whispered, "How . . ." Because nobody ever asked how Mr. Dante knew everything. He just did.

And he was kind enough to pretend he hadn't noticed her blunder.

So she didn't announce him or anything when he tapped on Princess Nicole's door and at the clear, "It's open!" entered.

She spoke into her two-way. "Bookman to see Hunter."

"Acknowledged."

Then she leaned against the wall, wondering what else was in store for the detail in the weeks to come. God knew, it had been a madhouse since the king got the famous letter.

She wondered what was in store for them all next, and found she couldn't wait to see.

That was the trick, the others had told her. That was how

they got you. They were a big, merry bunch of trouble-makers, and they pulled everyone into their madness.

Natalia checked to make sure the corridor was empty, then smiled, something that would have shocked the already shell-shocked palace inhabitants.

Chapter 50

Nicole was surprised to see a clearly rattled Mr. Dante walk into her room. At least she'd been in her room.

She'd gotten smart after her first visit to Jeff and went to the most diabolical source she knew.

Somehow, within twenty minutes, Nicky had procured a three-story rope ladder that would hold up to 320 pounds. So she no longer had to walk past Natalia when she returned; she just scurried back up the black ladder, which was downright invisible at night.

She was still wearing last night's outfit. Hopefully, Mr. Dante wouldn't notice.

Oh, who was she kidding? He noticed everything.

"Hi, Mr. Dante."

"Your Highness."

"You want something? Natalia rustles up a mean cup of coffee, no matter how many times I tell her to quit it."

"No, Highness."

She gestured for him to have a seat, but he ignored her. She couldn't help but be curious; what was he doing here? And what was wrong? "What's up?"

"I—ah—that is—the king—I have—I have been—"

"Whoa! You'd better sit down. You look like you've seen a ghost."

"Infinitely worse," he said darkly. "And I pray I never see such a sight again. Princess, I have been remiss."

She was having a hard time following the conversation. Well, it was early. And Edmund was clearly in the middle of a cerebral hemorrhage. "You've what now?"

"I neglected to explain the nature of your security detail."

"Okay."

"Do you think you're the only one who needed to leave the palace for an assignation?"

She stared at him. "Uh . . ."

"For one thing, do you think you would be here if royals couldn't sneak away for a little fun now and again?"

"That, um, hadn't occurred to—"

Wonder of wonders, he actually interrupted her. "Let your detail help you. If you wish to visit Jeffrey, Natalia will take you. And she would never tell the king. Just as the king would never—never mind."

There was no point in playing dumb, so she didn't bother. "But Jeffrey *is* my detail."

"Yes, that poses a problem, doesn't it?"

Suddenly she felt the urge to unburden herself. To tell him everything. She spoke to him like she would her mother. "He says while I'm in his apartment I'm just Nicole. But what about when he comes back from vacation? He won't be with me while he's on duty . . . and the detail considers themselves on duty twenty-four/seven."

"You mustn't begrudge them their devotion."

"Who's begrudging? It just makes my life more difficult, that's all."

"As opposed to what you're doing to Natalia," he said dryly.

"Hey! I didn't ask for any of this, and you know it."

"Tough nuts."

"And—what?"

"You didn't ask. You didn't want. You weren't ready. Nicole Krenski, are you a Princess of Alaska or are you a coward?"

"Call me that again," she said, "and spend the rest of the spring learning how to grow back your lungs."

"Then act like one, for pity's sake," he snapped. "One day, every man, woman, and child will depend upon you for their economy, the quality of their education, the health of the military budget. *Lives* will depend on the smallest decisions you make . . . or don't make."

"I'm not calming down, Mr. Dante."

He ignored her. "You fulfilled a dying wish. Then you agreed to a proper DNA test, knowing the consequences—I explained them to you myself. For better or for worse, you're here now. So be a Baranov, or not. But stop straddling the line."

He took a breath. She waited. Then, "You done?"

"I think so."

"Shit or get off the pot, huh?"

"You share your father's gift for the perfect turn of phrase. Also, fire Jeffrey."

"What?"

"Fire him. Then he will no longer feel conflicted between duty and desire. And you're a woman in your mid-thirties; you're entitled to take any lover you wish."

"I could never do that to him! His family's been doing this work for generations. It's all he knows."

"Then you have a problem. I suspect you will turn your mind toward solving it."

"Gee, thanks. Any other pearls of wisdom you want me to trip on?"

"None that come to mind," he admitted. "Please excuse me. I don't know what has gotten into me today."

"Hey, that's okay. Nobody's perfect."

"Least of all your father," he said cryptically, then marched out.

Chapter 51

"My God, woman, I think I threw my back out last night."

"Big Al, you don't fool me. Under all that bullshit is a big old teddy bear."

He was in his office chair and the Dragon was sitting on his lap, her feet dangling inches off the floor. "I think we took ten years off Edmund's life this morning."

"Well now, you were the one who wanted to try it with me on top."

"I told you, by then you'd already thrown my back out. What choice did I have?"

"Excuses, excuses. I wonder where this scene fits into my memoirs."

"Don't you dare!"

"Chapter fifteen," she mused, " 'I Bone The King.' "

"You're fired."

"You already fired me today."

"Well, you're fired again."

She ran her fingers through his graying hair. "Is that a fact?"

There was a rap on his door and he heard Alexandria call, "Dad? Can I come in?"

He shoved the Dragon off his lap and she went willingly enough. Then he yelled, "You harpy, get the hell out of my office!"

"Don't be like that, Big Al. All I want to know is how you met Princess Nicole's mother. You gotta admit that's historically significant."

"No way! There's historically significant and there's none of your damned business! Guess which this is?"

Alexandria walked in. "You two aren't fooling anyone. We all know you did the beast with two backs last night."

The king and the Dragon gaped at the princess.

"Well, we do," she said mildly, perching on the arm of one of the chairs. "Dad's detail knew, then Edmund knew, then the whole detail knew, and Nicky's been patching into their two-way since he learned how to hack, and he told all of us at breakfast, at which you were conspicuously absent, Dad, and I shudder to think why."

"Remind me to strangle my youngest," he said grimly.

"Hey, Dad. It's only such a big deal because we're happy for you. You've been alone too long." Alexandria, a breathtaking brunette with the standard-issue Baranov blue eyes, smiled at Holly. "Granted, your choice was kind of a surprise, but still . . ."

"No goddamned privacy in my own house," he grumped.

"Well, Dad. Did you think she kept coming back to write more deathless prose about signing the Conservation Act?"

"Why did everyone know why you kept coming back except me?"

"'Cuz you're a dumbass, Big Al."

"Do you want me to kick this broad out, Alex? Is this private business?"

"It is, but she'll have to know eventually. Get ready to be a grandfather again."

"Really?" He jumped up and swung his daughter around in a hug that left her breathless. Then, "Oh shit! Sorry. You're not gonna puke, are you?"

"Eventually, I imagine so."

"Congratulations, Alex," Holly said, smiling broadly.

"Just when I thought I couldn't take one more surprise, you lay this egg in my lap."

"Almost literally," Alex added, then giggled. "Another kid who'll think nothing of their grandpa being on all the money."

"How long have you—"

"Two days. I flew to the States to tell Sheldon, then hopped a transport back here. Shel will be here later today. Anyway, I'm due in November."

"Why'd you tell that bum first?"

"Because he's the father, Dad. I'm pretty sure. Kidding! Don't throw anything at me. In fact, I'll leave you two alone so you can have more old people sex." She shivered all over. "You know what? Maybe I will throw up." Then she left, closing the door firmly behind her.

"Congratulations, Grandpa," Holly said.

"If you ever call me Grandpa again, I'll fire you. Again."

"I think I'll chance it." She plopped back into his lap. "So, what's on today's agenda?"

"Fire. Brimstone. Worlds colliding. I mean, I'm doing the Dragon. Isn't that a sign of the Apocalypse?"

"Could be, Al," she laughed, leaning down and planting a kiss on his mouth. "Could be."

He started to kiss her back, then pulled away and looked her right in her big brown eyes. "I'm not getting married again, Holly. Never, ever again."

"Who's askin'?"

"So you'll never be queen."

"Who'd want the job?"

"And here I thought you were after me for my money. Or you were looking for a crown."

"Al, I'm after you, there's no doubt about that. Stop shivering! But your money and your crown don't have nothin' to do with it." She kissed him again. "You've got, ah, other qualities."

"What I've been saying," he said smugly.

Chapter 52

Natalia was escorting Nicole to the nearest coffee shop—she was hungry to get out of the palace—when her two-way beeped. She spoke into it, then turned to Nicole.

"Rebel wants to meet with you. It sounds urgent."

"Is he okay?"

"I don't know, Highness, but if he had been hurt, I would know."

"Okay. We'll go out some other time. Where is he?"

"His rooms."

"You'll have to take me there; I have no idea where they are."

"At once, Highness."

"Thanks, Natalia. Bet you can't wait until Jeff gets back."

"I'm counting the seconds, Highness."

"You're a weird one, Natalia."

"Thank you, Highness."

And in twenty minutes, she was knocking on Nicky's door.

"Nicky? It's Nicole. Okay if I come in?"

At the muffled, "Yeah," she turned the knob and entered.

The sixteen-year-old was clearly waiting for her; the television was off and he wasn't playing video games. Just sitting on the couch and waiting, his hands dangling in his lap. He was growing so quickly his cuffs were an inch above his wrists.

"What's up?"

"Dad's having sex again."

"You, um, didn't have to tell me that. *Ever.*"

"I think—I think he's ready to let my mother go."

"Okay. Listen, Nicky, I know it's awful and revolting to think about, but grown-ups have needs, even ancient doddering grown-ups like our father. It doesn't mean he loved your mother any less."

"I know. But I think he's officially over her now. So I can finally talk to you."

She sat down in the easy chair across from him. "Hon, I'm not up to a birds and bees chat. Last time was bad enough."

He snorted. "I'm sixteen, not six. I know all about sex."

"Really," she said, amused.

"But I wanted to show you this." He handed her a piece of paper, one that looked awfully familiar. She had seen one just like it not long ago, it was her—

"These are the results from *my* DNA test," Nicky explained.

"You—oh. How did you—"

"You've heard the rumors. Everybody has. Dad just won't hear them, and won't let anyone talk to me about them, or him. He was the guardian of her memory, I guess. But she's gone, and I'm too old to be taken care of anymore."

"I hear you on that last one," she said fervently, still trying to make sense of the numbers and words on the paper. "I'm thirty-five and I'm way *way* too old to be taken care of."

"Great, Nicole, and this is about me, not you."

"So sorry. Please continue."

"Anyway, Dr. Hedman had to take Dad's blood. And your blood. And then I cornered him and ordered him to take my blood and run the same test. See, always before, Dad wouldn't allow the test. He sure wouldn't cough up any of his blood for one."

"So you bullied Dr. Hedman—"

"I didn't *bully*," he corrected her sharply, sitting up straighter and looking like the prince he was. "I commanded. And he did as I asked. That piece of paper says I am not a blood relation to the king. None." He paused, obviously struggling to keep his composure. "My mother was a queen. And she was a liar and a betrayer."

Nicole bit her lower lip. "I see." She cleared her throat. "Well, two things. We can't ever know what was going on with Queen Dara. Maybe she fell in love. Maybe she was lonely. Maybe she made a mistake and was sorry later. Don't let that stupid piece of paper ruin your good memories of her. My—*our* father told me that the pain of a loved one's death goes away, leaving good memories. And that's what you have of your mom, Nicky. The good memories."

Impassively, he said, "You said two things."

"I'm sure you understand that in Dad's heart you'll be his son until the planets cave in on themselves."

He smiled thinly. "That's the second time."

"What?"

"The second time you've called him Dad since you came in here."

"Was it? I hadn't realized." Hmm. That *was* weird. It had sort of slipped out without her noticing.

"But see, it's okay."

"It is?"

"I've always felt like a changeling child, and now I know why. But it's okay. I think it was time for me to stop wondering and find out for sure. And I could only do that because of you. I think . . . I think I was meant to find out the king wasn't my father because part of me knew you were coming. With you here he still has the same number of children, you see."

"No, Nicky, he doesn't. He's got one more, that's all. Even if he knew, he'd never disown you, never cast you out. You're his son and that's all there is."

"I just don't know—" The boy clenched his fists and tried to lock back the tears. "I don't know what to do. I don't know if I should tell him or not. But since you went through this kind of thing not long ago, you're the only one I can talk to. The bastard princess. But what does that make me?"

"His son, Nicky. That's what it makes you. As for this?" She crumpled it in her fist and tossed it into the fireplace; then she got up, lit a match from the gold box on the mantel, and incinerated the DNA test into ash. "It's your business, Nicky, and no one else's. And I swear to you by *my* mother, I'll never tell. The bastard princess is a coward, but not a liar."

Nicky wiped his cheeks and said, surprised, "You're not a coward. I think you're very brave."

"Well, I'm not. But I'm going to try to be. Damned if I'll be shamed by a child."

"I'm *not* a—"

"I know, I know, sorry. Anyway, come on, *Prince* Nicky. I

was headed into town for coffee when you beeped Natalia, but now I feel the need for Dairy Queen. Let's go drown our sorrows in thousands of calories."

Shyly, he took her hand, and brother and sister left the suite of the youngest Baranov, the bastard prince.

Chapter 53

Jeffrey Rodinov rose in the middle of the morning with his mind made up. He shaved, showered, dressed, and called the super to report the damage Nicole had done to the sliding glass door.

Then he drove to the palace, found Edmund, and tendered his resignation.

"Absolutely not," was the reply, to his shock.

"Mr. Dante, there are circumstances—you don't understand—my duty is conflicting with—"

"The desire to impregnate Princess Nicole; yes; I gathered as much. Your resignation is *not* accepted."

"But sir! I—"

"I can't take it, Jeffrey; I absolutely can't take it!" Edmund (horrors!) yelled. Jeffrey thought, *The king died and nobody told me.* That's the only reason Edmund Dante would ever raise his voice or forget to comb his hair.

"Sir, maybe you'd better—"

"Go on a killing spree," he snapped. "I am surrounded by people having irresponsible sex!"

Shocked, Jeffrey had no reply.

Edmund visibly calmed himself. "Your resignation is not accepted. For heaven's sake, Jeffrey, look around you. This is Alaska. The royals marry subjects all the time. The greatest queen our country has ever seen used to be a maid. Also, there is no rule that says a princess may not bone her bodyguard."

Jeffrey was shocked into silence by Edmund's use of the word *bone* as a verb.

"Now, the king will give you nine kinds of holy hell about it, but that's your problem, not mine. Do you *see* the bags under my eyes, man? I cannot take another upheaval to the schedule. You will not quit."

"But Nicole—I mean, Her Highness—"

"—is at the Dairy Queen with the youngest prince. If you hurry, you can catch them."

Jeffrey turned, already groping in his pockets for his car keys. "With all respect, this isn't over, Mr. Dante."

"With zero respect, it certainly is, Jeffrey. Best of luck."

"Sir, are you all right?"

"I am a thousand yards from all right. Run along now."

Jeffrey ran along.

Jeffrey saw two detail automobiles parked in the driveway, and judging by all the citizens pressed to the windows, deduced Nicole was eating her ice cream inside one of the sedans.

He rapped on one dark window, which slowly slid down.

"Hi, Jeffrey!" Prince Nicholas called. Nicole was sitting beside her brother, closest to the window. "Want a cone? Is your vacation over already?"

"Yes," he said grimly.

"What are you doing here?" Nicole asked, clearly surprised.

"I'll get to that in a moment."

"Guess what?" Nicholas continued. "Dad's having sex and Alex is pregnant. And Christina's been such a bitch lately we think she is, too. Isn't that the most terrifying news you've ever heard?"

"Not this week, Highness. I—wait. The king is what?" He mentally shook himself. "Never mind. Please excuse me." He pressed a button on his two-way and the locks disengaged. Then he opened the door and yanked Nicole out.

"Hey! My Peanut Buster Parfait!"

He took her hand in his and led her to the other sedan, rapped on the driver's side window, and said to Natalia, "Out."

"Yes, sir." She got out.

"Don't talk to Natalia like that! Natalia, I'm sorry. He's an asshole."

"Yes, Your Highness."

"You. In."

Nicole took a steadying breath, shrugged, and climbed into the backseat. He turned to Natalia and said, "I'll need a few minutes of privacy."

"For what?" was her almost-but-not-quite-sarcastic request as he got in and shut and locked the doors.

"There's easier ways to get a bite of my parfait," she informed him. Then she was juggling the plastic tub of ice cream as he crushed her to him and kissed her until he thought he might bruise her. Then he eased up.

"Not that I mind, but this isn't exactly discreet, and I thought you were all about being—"

"Be my wife."

"Huh?"

"Marry me. Make me a prince."

"You mean you're in love with me for my title?" she teased, but he could tell she was rattled.

"All this time I've been coming at it from the wrong end."

She reddened. "If you're talking about what we tried

later last night, I told you, that happens to every guy now and—"

"I've been trying to reconcile my duty with one-night stands with the Crown Princess of Alaska. But I don't want a number of one-night stands, Nicole. I want you, for the rest of your life. And mine. Marry me and make me a prince, and as long as I'm by your side, you'll never want for family again."

"Actually," she said quietly, "I'm kind of getting used to them. My family."

"Oh." He felt his heart actually shrink in his chest. Of course, the famous Baranov bounce: They came back from every shock, every disaster, stronger than ever. He should have known. She didn't need him. She had never needed him.

And he was a fool.

"I see," he said stiffly, leaning away from her. "Then you have no need of me, or my proposal, so I—"

"Hold on, Jeffrey, I didn't say no, did I?"

"Nicole," he said stonily, "don't play with me like this."

"Who's playing? You're the one who keeps jumping to conclusions. Yes, I'll marry you. Yes, I'll make you a prince, and later, much much later by the grace of God, the King of Alaska."

She took another bite of her ice cream, chewed, and swallowed while his heart slowly resumed something resembling a normal rhythm. "You will? I mean, you do?"

"At first I thought it was because you didn't sulk after I got the drop on you that first day. Then I thought it was because you kept coming back to my old fishing guide job. Then I thought it was because you're really really good in bed. But now I think—"

"What?"

"I think," she said, pausing to lick the spoon, "it's because it's something my mother would have wanted for me. And I think it's because you're the best angler I've ever seen. I'm pretty sure I fell in love with you when I watched you tie on that sinker the day we went fishing."

He slumped back in the seat with relief. "Thank God."

Then he gathered her in his arms, ignoring her squealed, "I'm spilling my parfait!" and kissed her until they were both panting and covered with ice cream.

"By the way," he said, pulling back to catch his breath. "Who is the king having sex with?"

"Don't even ask, Jeffrey. You wouldn't believe it if I told you."

Chapter 54

"You're what?" the king screamed.

"Getting married. Oh, and having gobs of sex," Nicole added helpfully, ignoring Jeffrey's horrified groan.

"But you've only known each other a fucking week!"

"Funny *you* should use the word *fucking*. From what I hear—"

"Never mind about me, young lady."

"Young lady? Dad, I'm almost ready for bifocals."

"How can you possibly know—no offense, Jeff—how can you know this guy is the love of your life in a measly seven days?"

"Oh, I don't," she assured her father. "I'm marrying him for his great big dick."

The king and Jeffrey groaned in unison.

There was a knock on the door, and the king screamed, "Go away!"

"Uh, Dad? You okay in there?"

"Aw, fuck. Come in, David."

The prince entered cautiously. "Hi. What's—"

"Your sister has been boning her bodyguard like some awful American movie script she rewrote, and now she's got the idea in her teeny brain that she wants to marry him!"

David didn't miss a beat. "Really? Congratulations, Nicole. Welcome to the family, Jeffrey."

"No, no, no!"

"Dad, you're hardly in a position to—"

"Don't tell me what I'm in a position to or not to do. I'm the goddamned King of goddamned Alaska."

"Maybe you should get that on a T-shirt like Christina has," Nicole suggested, "because you seem to think nobody remembers."

"You guys, you're killing me." The king buried his face in his hands. "You're all out to get me. Don't think I don't know. I know things."

"Actually, David, I'm glad you're here. I really need to talk to you about something."

"You do, Nicole? Is there something you need help with? Because I—"

Another knock. "Big Al? You in there?"

"Go away!" he shouted. "Go away and die!"

The door opened and the Dragon sauntered in. "Aw, music to my ears, darlin'."

"Don't call me darlin', you horrible horrible thing. I'm having the worst week. No offense, Nicole. Jeffrey."

"None taken, Majesty."

"Don't you mean 'Dad'?" Nicole teased, laughing out loud as the king and Jeffrey flinched in unison.

"Looks like I missed all the excitement." The Dragon smelled news; she came into the room with her eyes wide and her ears perked up. "Congratulations."

"Don't congratulate them! I haven't given my permission yet."

"I don't need the permission of the sovereign and you know it," Nicole said coolly. "Neither of us do. This isn't England."

"Can't you pretend you're a little in awe of me?" the king begged.

"Aw, we all are, Big Al."

"You hush up. All you people are trying to drive me to a—"

"Also, I'm seriously thinking about abdicating to David."

The king pounded on his chest with a fist. "Ack! Here it comes! The fatal coronary!"

David turned to stare at her, ignoring his father's cries of distress. "You're what?"

"David, think about it. I'm not ready for this job. Dad's ancient, he could keel over any second. And there I'd be, jammed into a job I've had minimal training for. That's not good for the country."

"I'm keeling over right now!" the king gurgled.

"Although I think Jeffrey would make a fine king," Nicole added thoughtfully, nodding approvingly at the Dragon as she solicitously pounded the king on the back.

"No, I wouldn't," he replied. "I'm too used to seeing the job from the other side of the desk."

"That's *why* you'd—"

"Nicole, I thought we agreed we were going to spring these things on your father one at a time."

"You *planned* this? To assassinate me by speech?"

"I know, Jeffrey, but then David walked in and it was kind of the perfect moment to—"

"*Am I still in the goddamned room?*"

"Nicole." David was frowning at them. "I don't understand. You're the eldest. The crown is yours by right."

"Will you stop being so damn noble? I don't want it. Worse, I'm not ready for it. Even worse? I'm not worthy of it. You've got twenty IQ points on me, and more than thirty years of experience. There's no contest. At all."

"But you're the eldest," David repeated.

"I don't give a shit!"

"Hello, King of Alaska in the room. Maybe we should, I don't know, PRETEND I'M IN CHARGE AND DISCUSS IT WITH ME?"

It took twenty seconds for everyone's ears to stop ringing. And when they did, it was the Dragon who spoke. "I know how to settle this."

"Don't listen to her," Al warned. "She's dangerously insane."

"I think you should take care of this the American way."

"What? Have a revolution? Loosen the gun laws? What?"

"Have a poll. Ask the Alaskan people who *they* want running their lives when Al kicks it."

"But this isn't a democracy," David said.

"Yeah, an' you know how many monarchies aren't around anymore because people decided family lineage was no way to decide who ran the country? I could give you a list. Hell, David, you could probably give me one. So why don't you put it out there for the people? I'm not saying you should let 'em decide. But the figures might help y'all decide what's really best for the country."

They argued. They swore at each other. The king disinherited Nicole, then fired Jeffrey, then disinherited David. The Dragon laughed her ass off. The king begrudgingly took it all back.

Then Nicole asked the Dragon, "How *does* one conduct a poll, anyway?"

Part Three

PRINCESS NICOLE KRENSKI

Chapter 55

BASTARD PRINCESS GIVES FIRST PRESS CONFERENCE
ANNOUNCES LEGAL TITLE TO THE WORLD
ABDICATES THRONE TO CROWN PRINCE DAVID

"So that's what it is?" Nicholas asked. "Your title is HRH Princess Nicole Krenski? Like Krenski was your middle name?"

"It's the best way I can reconcile my Baranov side with my mother's memory. I know the general consensus around here is that she was selfish to keep me to herself her entire life, but the bottom line is, I owe everything to her."

"Nobody at this table," the king said mildly, pretending it was a comment and not a command (no one was fooled), "has one bad thing to say about your dear mother."

"Agreed," David said. He raised his water glass. "To Ms. Krenski, mother of the bastard princess."

The other siblings and in-laws raised their glasses and thundered "To Ms. Krenski!" so loud the chandelier tinkled.

"And you'll never ever be queen?" Nicky persisted.

"God willing," Nicole said fervently. "David's cut out for

it. I'm not. Everybody at the table was nice to pretend otherwise."

There was an awkward silence, broken by, "Jeffrey, will you stop standing in the corner and go eat lunch with your fiancée?" the king demanded. "You're not on her detail anymore."

"With all respect, Your Majesty, I am until the wedding day."

The king brightened. "Then that means—I knew your father, and your grandfather, so that means—"

"No sex until I'm a married woman," Nicole said glumly. "Fucking sense of duty."

"Language, kiddo."

"Hey, am I the eldest or am I the eldest?" she demanded, smiling up at the footman who refilled her milk glass.

"Trust me," David said, "you don't get any special treatment. And you've got to put up with gobs of annoying younger sibs."

Kathryn sneered and threw a buttered roll at her brother, who, from years of practice, ducked handily.

"Y'all's dinner manners remind me o' this family of monkeys I saw in a zoo once. The head monkey, who was by far the smelliest—"

"That's it, Dragon. You're fired!"

"Let me finish my soup, at least. Christina made it herself. Tastes like spring, darlin'," she added to Christina.

"Thanks. Listen, Nicole, I feel terrible that we got off on the wrong foot. I know what it's like to lose a mother. I just—" To everyone's shock, she burst into tears. "I handled it all wrong and I'm *so* sorry!"

"Jeez, stop it, okay, okay, I forgive you." Nicole had rarely been so alarmed. On the whole, she preferred her sister-in-law to come out of the corner swinging, not sobbing. "It's not a big deal. We're family, right?"

"Yes, yes, we are! And, Holly, I love you. I really really love you. Al's been alone too long."

"We're not discussing my sex life at the dinner table," the king commanded.

"Sorry, Al, I—" Christina grabbed her napkin . . . and threw up in it.

"Oh, guh-ross!" Kathryn and Nicholas screamed in unison.

"Hey, I almost barfed myself. *I* sure don't want to discuss Dad's sex life," Nicole said.

"My wife is indisposed," David sighed. "Honey, I think it's way past time you went to the doctor."

"You mean I have to share my first pregnancy with Pregzilla?" Alexandria demanded as her husband, Shel, laughed like a hyena. "Chris, how late are you?"

"Five weeks," she mumbled, accepting with thanks several clean napkins.

"See? Not fair! I'm two weeks behind you! You're gonna be first . . . again!"

"What the hell are you bitching about?" Alexander-the-younger snapped. "The rest of us are putting up with *two* pregnant sociopaths."

Nicole caught Jeffrey's eye and winked. Without changing expression, he winked back.

They were noisy. They were obnoxious. She had zero privacy. She had less solitude. There was a new emergency every day.

She sighed happily and buttered another roll.

The bastard princess was home at last.

A Note to the Reader

This will very likely be the last Alaskan Royal book. When I first pitched the idea to my editor ("What if Alaska was its own country, with a weirdo royal family?"), I had no idea I was pitching a trilogy.

This all came about when my husband and I visited Juneau for our tenth wedding anniversary. I came away from the state with great admiration for the locals, not to mention being utterly staggered by the sheer beauty of the place. It was like being stuck in a gorgeous postcard for an entire week. And it was difficult to leave.

While I was there, I bought up every book on Alaskan history I could find, and once I plowed through them all, I had the beginning of an idea. See, until I read those books I had no idea that we came *this close* to not buying Alaska. We were in the middle of the Civil War at the time, and the last thing the Union wanted was another state it might not be able to control.

That was the moment for most writers: the "what-if" moment. What if we hadn't bought Alaska? What if it remained under Russian control until a bunch of rebels overthrew their Russian overlords and took the place for themselves? How would that affect the state-that-was-now-a-country? How would it affect America? And what would Alaskan royalty be like?

So I pitched what I thought would be a stand-alone book, *The Royal Treatment.* But it seemed quite a few readers enjoyed reading about the parallel universe I plucked from my brain, a world where Martha Stewart never saw the inside of a prison cell and where the Twin Towers still proudly stood. A world where it was possible to be a princess in blue jeans. Where kings went fishing as often as they signed bills into law. A world where being royalty was not synonymous with inbred weakness.

At the urging of readers, I came up with another tale, and now I'll be wrapping up the loose ends with book number three.

For those of you who have followed these books, thank you. For those who prefer the Betsy books, there's still quite a few of those on the drawing board. But if you're fond of the series and don't wish it to end, don't despair. Who could stop the Alaskan Royals from being heard if they really want to be?

Not I.
